Praise for Cars

Trial by Fi

"My favourite Carsen Taite books are the [...] as a criminal defense lawyer shows. This one falls into that category. Everything about the MCs' jobs was exciting, the inner workings of the courthouse, the atmosphere, the differences between the PD office and Wren's high profile law firm but also the differences between the PD office and the DA office. The way the philosophies clash yet both offices need the other, two sides of the Justice coin. Taite's insider knowledge shows in tiny details, and I would happily have read more about cases and untangling facts and lies to reach as much of the truth as possible."—*Jude in the Stars*

Her Consigliere

"With this sexy lesbian romance take on the mobster genre, Taite brings savvy, confidence, and glamour to the forefront without leaning into violence...Taite's protagonists ooze competence and boldness, with strong female secondary characters...This is sure to please."
—*Publishers Weekly*

"Siobhan and Royal have wonderful chemistry from the first time they meet. Carsen Taite writes the irresistibility very well, the powerlessness of the head over what heart and body desire...Carsen Taite is always a sure bet, her stories always entertaining. This one is no exception."
—*Les Rêveur*

Spirit of the Law

"I would definitely recommend this to romance fans and those that like their romance to include lawyers and a little bit of mystery. Due to the slight paranormal elements I think paranormal romance fans would also enjoy this even if they don't normally read Taite."—*LGBTQ Reader*

Best Practice

"I had fun reading this story and watching the final law partner find her true love. If you like a delightful, romantic age-gap tale involving lawyers, you will like *Best Practice*. In fact, I believe you will like all three books in the Legal Affairs series."—*Rainbow Reflections*

Out of Practice

"Taite combines legal and relationship drama to create this realistic and deeply enjoyable lesbian romance…The reliably engaging Taite neatly balances romance and red-hot passion with a plausible legal story line, well-drawn characters, and pitch-perfect pacing that culminates in the requisite heartfelt happily-ever-after."—*Publishers Weekly*

Practice Makes Perfect

"This book has two fantastic leads, an attention-grabbing plot and that sizzling chemistry that great authors can make jump off the page. While all of Taite's books are fantastic, this one is on that next level. This is a damn good book and I cannot wait to see what is next in this series."
—*Romantic Reader Blog*

Outside the Law

"[A] fabulous closing to the Lone Star Law series…Tanner and Sydney's journey back to each other is sweet, sexy and sure to keep you entertained."—*Romantic Reader Blog*

A More Perfect Union

"Readers looking for a mix of intrigue and romance set against a political backdrop will want to pick up Taite's latest novel."—*RT Book Reviews*

Reasonable Doubt

"Another Carsen Taite novel that kept me on the edge of my seat…[A]n interesting plot with lots of mystery and a bit of thriller as well. The characters were great."—*Danielle Kimerer, Librarian, Reading Public Library*

Lay Down the Law

"Recognized for the pithy realism of her characters and settings drawn from a Texas legal milieu, Taite pays homage to the prime-time soap opera *Dallas* in pairing a cartel-busting U.S. attorney, Peyton Davis, with a charity-minded oil heiress, Lily Gantry."—*Publishers Weekly*

Courtship

"Taite keeps the stakes high as two beautiful and brilliant women fueled by professional ambitions face daunting emotional choices…

As backroom politics, secrets, betrayals, and threats race to be resolved without political damage to the president, the cat-and-mouse relationship game between Addison and Julia has the reader rooting for them. Taite prolongs the fever-pitch tension to the final pages. This pleasant read with intelligent heroines, snappy dialogue, and political suspense will satisfy Taite's devoted fans and new readers alike."
—*Publishers Weekly*

Beyond Innocence

"Taite keeps you guessing with delicious delay until the very last minute…Taite's time in the courtroom lends *Beyond Innocence* a terrific verisimilitude someone not in the profession couldn't impart. And damned if she doesn't make practicing law interesting."—*Out in Print*

The Best Defense

"Real-life defense attorney Carsen Taite polishes her fifth work of lesbian fiction, *The Best Defense*, with the realism she daily encounters in the office and in the courts. And that polish is something that makes *The Best Defense* shine as an excellent read."—*Out & About Newspaper*

Nothing but the Truth

"Author Taite is really a Dallas defense attorney herself, and it's obvious her viewpoint adds considerable realism to her story, making it especially riveting as a mystery. I give it four stars out of five."—*Bob Lind, Echo Magazine*

Do Not Disturb

"Taite's tale of sexual tension is entertaining in itself, but a number of secondary characters…add substantial color to romantic inevitability."—*Richard Labonte, Book Marks*

It Should Be a Crime—Lammy Finalist

"Taite, a criminal defense attorney herself, has given her readers a behind the scenes look at what goes on during the days before a trial. Her descriptions of lawyer/client talks, investigations, police procedures, etc. are fascinating. Taite keeps the action moving, her characters clear, and never allows her story to get bogged down in paperwork. *It Should Be a Crime* has a fast-moving plot and some extraordinarily hot sex."
—*Just About Write*

By the Author

Romances

Truelesbianlove.com

It Should Be a Crime

Do Not Disturb

Nothing but the Truth

The Best Defense

Beyond Innocence

Rush

Courtship

Reasonable Doubt

Without Justice

Sidebar

A More Perfect Union

Love's Verdict

Pursuit of Happiness

Leading the Witness

Drawn

Double Jeopardy
(novella in Still Not Over You)

Spirit of the Law

Her Consigliere

The Luca Bennett Mysteries:

Slingshot

Battle Axe

Switchblade

Bow and Arrow
(novella in Girls with Guns)

Lone Star Law Series:

Lay Down the Law

Above the Law

Letter of the Law

Outside the Law

Legal Affairs Romances

Practice Makes Perfect

Out of Practice

Best Practice

Courting Danger Romances:

Trial by Fire

Trial and Error

Visit us at www.boldstrokesbooks.com

TRIAL AND ERROR

by

Carsen Taite

2022

ISBN 13: 978-1-63555-863-0

This Trade Paperback Original Is Published By
Bold Strokes Books, Inc.
P.O. Box 249
Valley Falls, NY 12185

First Edition: June 2022

Credits
Editor: Cindy Cresap
Production Design: Stacia Seaman
Cover Design by Tammy Seidick

Acknowledgments

I don't think I'll ever get tired of revisiting my old stomping ground, the Dallas County Courthouse, and being able to do so in the pages of this series is a gift. Thanks for indulging my love of the law and the people who work hard to find balance in a world that often seems off kilter.

Thanks to everyone at Bold Strokes Books for giving my stories a home and treating them with such care. Huge thanks to my smart, funny, and very patient editor, Cindy Cresap. Tammy, thank you for the striking covers for this entire series.

Putting the words on paper might be a solitary pursuit, but I couldn't do it without the support of my amazing group of friends. Georgia—thanks for our daily check-ins. When I'm not on track, I always know I can turn to you for encouragement, and your friendship is a treasure. Hugs to Ruth, Melissa, Kris, Elle, and Ali. Paula—you're the best bestie a girl could have and I'm ever grateful for your willingness to talk through tangled plot points and read pages way into the night. Thanks for being my ride or die.

Thanks to my wife, Lainey, for always believing in my dreams and always being willing to leap toward the next adventure.

And to you, dear reader, thank you for taking a chance on my work and coming back for more. You're the best!

To Lainey and a life full of love and adventure.

CHAPTER ONE

Franco Rossi pulled the phone away from her ear and stared at the screen. She didn't recognize the number and she couldn't make out anything the caller was saying through the sobs on the other end of the line. Julie, her assistant, guarded her cell number like it was a combination to a safe full of cash, which meant either this was someone who'd made it past the gatekeeper or a random crank call. She was about to write it off as the latter when one word pierced the jagged cries.

"...murder..."

"Hang on," Franco said, pulling her car into the nearest parking lot. She glanced at the clock on her dashboard, noting she had about ten minutes to spare before she'd be late for her hearing. She injected her voice with the well-practiced, soothing tone that had landed her a spot in the top ten attorneys in Houston. "I would like to help you, but I need you to speak slowly and clearly. Are you in trouble?"

A whimper and the snort of a blown nose was the first response followed by a whispered, "Yes, but not for me. It's for my son, Devon." A pause and then she cleared her throat. "Franco, it's Jenna. Jenna Grant. Tell me you remember me. Please."

Shit. She remembered all right. The vivid memories of her

youth flashed before her eyes in bright high-definition color before fading back into the darkness. She shoved her thoughts away and settled on a simple response. "I know who you are."

A few beats of silence followed, and she prayed the line had disconnected or that Jenna lost her number or that the call had never happened.

"Franco, are you there?"

Jenna's pleading tone pushed past her dread, and Franco closed her eyes to contemplate her options, none of which were good. There was only one right thing to do even if it was the last thing she wanted. "What do you need?" She braced for Jenna's response.

"Devon, my son. He's a freshman at Richards. A good kid. Paying his own way. Never in trouble."

Franco took in the staccato bullet points and digested them one by one. Jenna had a college age son—were they really that old? Devon might follow in his mother's footsteps, attend the same college, pay his own way, but as for the rest? Jenna had never been a good kid and she'd certainly gotten into plenty of trouble. "Are you married?" The question tumbled out before she could stop it.

"What?" Jenna asked distractedly. "No. No, I'm not married. Can we get back to Devon?"

Franco resisted pointing out that she was trying to circle back to that very topic with questions about Devon's dad. "Of course. What's going on?"

"Devon was arrested last week and charged with murdering his girlfriend."

The words dropped like boulders, and Franco struggled to digest what she was hearing. Her first instinct was to comfort Jenna, tell her everything would be okay, but comforting words were what she doled out to clients and friends, and Jenna was neither. "Why are you telling me this?"

"I've kept up with you," Jenna said. "Not like a stalker, but just out of whatever might be left of our friendship. You're one of the best lawyers in the state."

The compliment hung in the air and Franco wasn't sure how to respond. She *was* one of the best lawyers in the state, and she spent her days on her feet, challenging opposing counsel and judges to get justice for her clients, never holding back and never at a loss for words. Why was it when a ghost from her past reappeared, she suddenly had no idea what to say?

Because simply hearing Jenna's voice on the phone took her back in time and she could almost feel the crush of their circumstance coming back to steal her dreams. She shook her head, and then realized she had to actually verbalize her thoughts because Jenna wasn't right here in front of her.

"I can send you some names."

"Of attorneys in Dallas?"

The name of one particular attorney in Dallas sprang to Franco's mind, but she wasn't ready to say her name out loud. "Yes. I know a few."

"Don't you think I already tried to find someone on my own? I'm not completely helpless. Believe it or not, you were not my first call."

"Who was?"

"Excuse me?"

"You heard me. Who was your first call if it wasn't me?" Franco braced for the answer.

Jenna sighed. "Yes, I called her first, but Nina won't help me. She wouldn't even take my call."

"I find that hard to believe."

"Don't. It's a long story, but we haven't spoken in years."

Franco idly wondered why Jenna was on the outs with Nina, but their shared friendship was too distant for it to make any difference in her current life, and she'd vowed long ago not to live in the past. But her head filled with imagined pictures of present-day Nina, telling her secretary she wasn't interested in talking to Jenna. She imagined Nina had a secretary, but she didn't really know anything about Nina's practice, having purposely avoided following Nina's career since she graduated from law school. In her head she imagined Nina in a big office, in a shiny downtown building. She probably practiced some version of transactional law where she spent her days helping her clients acquire things, sell things—anything that didn't involve significant controversy or drama. She'd be wearing fancy suits and driving expensive cars, but she was still down-to-earth, endearing her to even the hardest-hearted CEOs.

Franco wanted to linger with her made-up version of Nina's world, but Jenna's voice pushed its way into her peace again. "Franco?"

"Yes?"

"He's a good kid. He didn't do this. His girlfriend is…was the daughter of Harry Benton. Surely even in Houston, you've heard of Benton Enterprises."

"I have," Franco said, her stomach tightening at the mention of the billionaire oil tycoon, real estate developer, and philanthropist for conservative causes.

"Then you'll understand when I say no one here wants to touch the case. I really need you. Devon really needs you. I don't have a lot of money, but I could take out a second mortgage to pay your fee. I know it's last minute, but he has a bond hearing on Friday. Please just meet him and then I promise I'll work out the details. I don't expect any handouts from you."

Her last words stung a bit, but the desperate plea before the dig stirred something in Franco. An underdog. A challenge. How long had it been since she'd experienced the thrill of an uphill climb? She'd lived for that buzz at the beginning of her career when her own experience drove her to take any case, no matter how unwinnable everyone else thought it was. But now her life was full of carefully curated clients for whom every difficulty could be overcome with enough resources, and for whom she'd calculated the very best odds, made easier to predict when money was no object. She was able to hire the very best experts and a team of jury consultants. On her last case, she'd even employed a professional trained in reading micro expressions. She gamed at the highest level and there were no more underdogs, only well-armed soldiers ready to battle from a position of strength.

Her life's work had become boring and predictable.

She started typing on her phone before practicality caused her to change her mind. "I'm texting you my assistant's email address. Send her whatever information you have about Devon's case so far, and I'll think about it."

She clicked off the line before Jenna could say anything else, but too late, she realized she'd used Devon's name, personalizing him and his case. She told herself she'd look over whatever Jenna sent and that was it, but she knew she wouldn't stop there. There was no substitute for being on the ground, in the place where it happened, to determine the best course of action, if there was one.

Franco rolled the thought over in her head. On the ground meant going back to Dallas, the city she'd largely left behind, aside from infrequent and awkward visits with her dad. Any more frequent contact only dredged up bittersweet memories of all she'd left behind. For years, she'd managed to keep the memories at bay, refusing to be distracted by the things that could've been, yet the reminders were still there, nipping at the edge of her consciousness. The moment she answered the call from Jenna, the nipping had turned into full-fledged gnawing, and there was only one way to make it stop. Before she could change her mind, she clicked on the speed dial button she used countless times a day, and when Julie answered she spoke fast to keep from changing her mind. "Clear my schedule for the rest of the week. I'm going to Dallas."

CHAPTER TWO

Nina Aguilar searched her desk for the files for the morning docket, finally finding them underneath a stack of papers she was supposed to fill out before the annual budget meeting at the end of the week. Between crunching numbers and covering Judge Larabee's docket while he was on medical leave, she was completely swamped, and she'd be glad when Hannah, her court coordinator, was back from maternity leave because the mountain of paperwork was becoming insurmountable in her absence. She took a moment to thumb through the files and make sure they matched the list on the docket. Satisfied she was as ready as possible to handle the double duty day, she stood and reached to pull her robe off the hook by her desk. She was holding it aloft in her outstretched hand when she heard a voice from across the room.

"Are you going to stare at it or put it on?"

She turned, pleased to see her best friend, Lennox Roy, standing in the doorway of her office. "Jury's still out on that one." She gestured from her neck to her hemline. "I mean, have you seen this suit? It seems a shame to cover it up."

Lennox nodded slowly. "True. You should probably resign your bench and go into practice so everyone can bear witness to your amazing fashion sense." She squinted and made a show of shielding her eyes. "It's really, really red."

"'Really, really red'?" Nina sighed. "I can tell when you're mocking me, and you really shouldn't mock me today."

Lennox pulled out her phone and acted like she was ready to compose a text. "Tell me what day I'm supposed to mock you, and I'll clear my schedule."

"Hilarious. I bought it for election night, but it's been hanging in my closet for a couple of weeks now, begging me to wear it. Besides, it's probably bad luck to buy a winning suit before voting even starts, right?"

"As if you aren't a shoo-in," Lennox said. "Seriously, you should go ahead and treat yourself to another suit. Buy all the suits, I say. As long as you don't make me go shopping with you," she added with a grin.

Nina returned the grin and tossed the robe onto her chair. "Speaking of treating." She reached into her desk drawer, pulled out a box, and handed it to Lennox, barely able to stand the anticipation. "Congratulations on your first day as super chief. This is just a little something to commemorate the occasion. I mean you should probably have a cape or something to go with the moniker. Who came up with the whole 'super chief' title anyway?"

"Your rambling is adorable." Lennox shook the box. "What is it?" She shook it harder. "Nothing breakable, I hope."

Nina laughed. "I know you better than that. It's a fancy pen, but not so fancy that you'll die if you lose it. Sorry to spoil the surprise, but I've got a full docket and I'm already behind because one of the elevators from the jail broke down."

"Tell me about it. I came down here to watch you roast Henderson on his first open plea, and everyone's sitting around in the courtroom waiting on the defendant."

"I don't roast new prosecutors," Nina said. "That's your new job. I merely make sure justice is fairly applied, and sometimes that requires me to be a hard-ass."

"Whatever." Lennox opened the box and grinned when she saw the copper fountain pen etched in Ruth Bader Ginsburg quotes. "This is gorgeous and I promise not to lose it, but can I stow this in your office until after the hearing?"

A knock on the slightly ajar door interrupted their conversation and Wren Bishop from the public defender's office stuck her head in the door. "Did you give her the pen?" Wren asked. She gasped and put a hand over her mouth. "Sorry. I didn't mean to spoil the surprise."

"No worries," Nina said. "The gift-giving portion of the morning is complete, and you're free to pilfer the contents of her box." Nina played the words back in her head and instantly felt the heat of her cheeks blush.

"That's what she said," Wren said, her face fixed into a neutral expression for a moment before she burst out laughing. "Sorry, Judge."

Nina smiled at her best friend's girlfriend. "How many times do I have to say it's Nina, especially when we're outside the courtroom. And, I think after a comment like that, you should definitely be calling me by my first name."

"Copy that." Wren pointed at the door. "My client's down from the jail, and we're ready to get started whenever you are."

Nina sighed and tugged on the robe. "Tell Marty I'll be right there," she said, referring to her bailiff. This plea had been on the books for a while now. The case had originally been set for trial, scheduled to start tomorrow, but in a surprise move, the defendant, Walt Ferguson, had agreed to an open plea, which meant he'd enter a plea of guilty and basically throw himself on the mercy of the court, with Wren presenting evidence why he deserved a lighter punishment than ADA Henderson was willing to offer. He was the first of three defendants who'd been arrested in a spree of violence, and one more was still at large. What happened today would set the tone for how the rest of the cases were resolved.

"Will do," Wren said and disappeared as quickly as she'd shown up.

"She's a keeper," Nina said.

Lennox grinned. "I know, right?"

"And she's probably going to eat your young prosecutor for lunch out there."

"We'll see."

"How are things working out for you two, working on opposite sides all the time?"

"We're only on opposite sides at work, and now that I'm chief instead of grinding it out in a court, we'll have a lot less chance of winding up in a direct standoff. It's a dance and she's a great lead."

Nina locked arms with Lennox and pulled her into a hug. "Look at you, being all sweet and deferential to your girlfriend. Who are you, by the way?"

Lennox shrugged. "Don't make a big deal out of it."

"That's the Lennox I know," Nina said. "Or a slightly less surly version, anyway." It made her feel good to see her best friend finally happy and settled in a relationship. And if she had to admit it, she was a little jealous of the relationship part. "You sure Wren doesn't have a sister?"

"Don't you have a plea to take?"

"Fine. Come on." Nina led the way out of her office. When they reached the hallway, Lennox split off to the left. Nina hated this part. She'd spent years here as a prosecutor, but even after several years as a judge, she wasn't used to having to go her own way, to the door in the opposite direction that led directly to her elevated seat behind the bench in the corner of the courtroom. She started to head in that direction, but abruptly changed her mind and followed Lennox through the other door that led into the well of the courtroom. Marty, her bailiff, was standing right by the door when she pushed through, and he looked surprised to see her.

"Good morning, Judge. The defendant is finally here."

Nina looked over at a young man dressed in a white jumpsuit sitting at the defense counsel table. "He's a lot younger than I expected."

Marty shook his head. "Sorry, that's Devon Grant, one of the cases from Larabee's docket. Bond hearing. I had him out here because we're kind of crammed back there right now." He pointed at the door to the holdover. "I can put Devon up if you want me to go ahead and bring Ferguson out."

Nina glanced at Wren and Henderson. "Counselors, are you ready to start?"

Wren spoke an enthusiastic yes, but Nina could see the look of abject terror in Henderson's eyes and she decided to cut him a break. She turned to Marty. "I don't recall seeing the file on Grant. Who's handling that one?"

He consulted his clipboard. "Sorry about that. It's one of Larabee's and it got lost in the shuffle, but the file's up there," he said, pointing at the bench on the other side of the room. "Defense attorney stepped out of the room—not anyone I know. Rigley's the prosecutor on the case and he's in the DA workroom talking to the victim's father. Considering who it is, I thought you might want to get this one over with first." He leaned in and whispered the next words. "Victim was Lacy Benton."

Crap. She looked over at the gallery of the courtroom, for the first time noticing the press lined up in the back of the room. Lacy Benton's murder was still grabbing headlines a week after the arrest of her boyfriend, likely because her father, Harry Benton, was a bigwig in the oil industry and one of the most generous philanthropists in Dallas. He was brash and ruthless and showy, and she was glad now that she hadn't seen his daughter's file on her docket today or she might've decided to stay in chambers rather than start her day with what was sure to be a dumpster fire of a hearing featured on the evening news.

She made a split-second decision that the best thing to do was get the bond hearing over with as soon as possible. "Go ahead and bring Mr. Ferguson out, but let's do the bond hearing first. Tell Rigley he's got three minutes to get in here and, if he has any witnesses, they better be ready. And send someone to get the defense attorney."

She told Wren and Henderson not to go anywhere, that their hearing would be next. Determined to make the best of this day despite the curveball that had just been thrown her way, she took a deep breath and started to turn away when the rear door of the courtroom opened and a woman walked through, immediately capturing her attention.

It had been nineteen years, and Nina didn't think she'd ever seen Franco in a suit, but she'd recognize the confident bearing and the strong set of her jaw anywhere, anytime. She lingered for a moment, waiting to see if Franco would look her way. She tried not to stare as one, two, three seconds passed—an agonizing delay. As if she'd been following the countdown, Franco slowly turned toward her, and they locked gazes. Franco had the same wavy dark hair she remembered and Nina recognized the deep, dark, brown eyes, as if only days had passed since their last meeting. Memories flooded her mind. Should she say something? Should she turn and walk away?

Rooted in place, she decided walking away wasn't a viable option, so she raised her hand tentatively and watched as Franco's eyes narrowed and then widened with recognition.

Nina started to call out to her, but before she could get the words out, the doors to the courtroom opened again, and almost immediately she heard a loud pop, followed by another, but until she saw the first body fall, she had no idea what was happening.

CHAPTER THREE

Thirty minutes earlier

Franco walked through the door of the courtroom and lingered at the back for a moment. The room itself wasn't unlike those in Harris County, which meant it looked the same as the ones she was used to, and judging by the various groups of attorneys huddled together in animated conversation, it might be just as cliquish as well. Being the out-of-towner was never easy, even when it came to big city courthouses.

"Help you find something?"

She turned toward the crusty older bailiff and offered him what she hoped was a winning smile. "I hope so. I'm here for a bond hearing on Devon Grant's case. I thought it was assigned to the 265th, but when I showed up there this morning, they sent me over here."

He nodded. "That's right. Judge Larabee is going to be out for an extended leave, so all of his cases have been reassigned." He consulted a clipboard in his hand. "Yep, you're in the right place." He pointed at the door to the holdover. "We've got a full house today, but I can give you five minutes with him before things get started."

Franco smiled in gratitude for the concession. "That would be great. Thanks."

She followed his lead and stepped into the tiny space behind the door where attorneys were standing in front of a small bank of plexiglass windows, each one speaking louder than the others in order to be heard over the din. She waited off to the side while the bailiff disappeared through another door only to emerge a moment later with a prisoner in tow. While he motioned for the inmate to take a seat in a chair in the corner of the room, Franco made a few mental notes. Even at nineteen, Devon Grant was way younger-looking than she'd expected. He was practically swimming in his jail-issued jumpsuit, but the big thing that jumped out at her was the abject fear in his eyes that said, "How did I wind up here and how do I get out?"

Quit projecting. He might be guilty.

She shrugged away the thought and focused on using the next few minutes as wisely as possible. "Devon, my name is Franco Rossi. I'm an attorney, and your mother asked me to meet with you and handle your bond hearing."

"I didn't do it."

She took a deep breath and injected her voice with as much calm reassurance as she could muster. "That's a great start, but not why we're here today. This hearing is to request that the judge lower your bond to a more reasonable amount— one that will allow your mom to post bail so that you can get out and be in a better position to work with your attorney to defend your case."

He nodded, but then cocked his head. "Wait. What do you mean 'your attorney'? Isn't that what you are?"

His voice rose on the last few words, like panic was rushing in, but she couldn't focus on that right now since they only had a few more minutes before their time was up. "I'm your attorney today. Once you get out, we'll have a real meeting where we can talk in private and decide if we're a good fit for each other for the long haul. Okay?"

"Okay."

The tremor in his voice told her his grip on calm was tenuous at best. "Your mom says you've never been in trouble before. Do you have a job?"

"I did, but I quit when school started."

"And you're in your first semester at Richards?"

"Yeah. I'm on a scholarship." His eyes widened. "Do you think I'm going to lose it?"

Memories rushed in again, but she batted them away. "One thing at a time. Everything will be easier to manage when you're out of here. Your mom says you pledged a fraternity. Do you live at the house?"

"Yes, but I barely moved in."

"Will any of your brothers vouch for you?"

"Maybe. I can make a list of them, but all their numbers are in my phone."

"That's okay. We'll do that after the hearing."

"Don't you want to hear my side of this?"

"Absolutely. We'll talk at length, but not here." She glanced around at the crowded space, willing him to read the room. She wasn't entirely sure they'd ever get into the nitty-gritty of the case. She was doing this hearing as a favor to Jenna, but covering a bond hearing and defending a murder case were two very different things and there was a lot to sort out before she committed to the full ride. He didn't need to know that though. Right now, all Devon needed was to get through the next hour without losing his shit. She patted him on the knee.

"Here's how this is going to go. The prosecutor may call some witnesses to say why they think you should have a high bail and it will look like the judge is listening to them and taking what they say into consideration, but the bottom line is that unless you are a flight risk and don't have adequate protection in place to ensure you come back to court for all of your scheduled appearances, the exorbitant bond the magistrate assigned at the jail is not warranted. The bond will probably still be a bit high because it's a murder case, but I'm confident it will be reduced significantly. I'll do all the talking. Okay?"

He lifted his chin and stared her square in the face. "Okay."

The bailiff strode over to them. "I'm moving him to the courtroom because we're getting too crowded back here. You can finish talking to him out there."

Franco didn't have anything else to say, but she knew Devon would want to continue the conversation, trying to convince her he was innocent and that's why she should do her best work for him. She couldn't blame him, but she didn't want to have any substantive conversation with him out where everyone could hear. "Sounds good. I'm going to step out into the hall and see if I can find his mother and I'll be right back."

The bailiff led Devon out the door and pointed to the back of the courtroom. "If you want to talk to the ADA on the case, his office is right back there."

"Are you always this friendly to out-of-towners?"

"Nope." He grinned. "But I usually give everyone a chance before I make judgments about whether they know what they're doing. You look like you know your way around a case."

She returned his grin and wondered what he saw in her that gave him that impression. It was true, she'd appeared as an attorney in every major courthouse in this state except for this one, but that was by choice, not happenstance. She hoped she wouldn't regret her decision to show up here today, but she wasn't holding her breath.

She made her way back to the DA's office where the door was open. Two people, a man and a woman, were seated at desks on opposite sides of the tiny room. Definitely junior prosecutors. She glanced at the closed door in the back of the room and surmised the chief for this court was probably in a meeting. There were already several defense attorneys camped out in the tiny space, so she decided to go back into the courtroom and wait there. On her way out of the room, she felt her phone buzz in her pocket. She fished it out and sighed when she saw Jenna's name on the screen, and she stepped into the hallway to take the call. "Where are you? I'm about to meet with Devon."

Jenna sighed. "I'm stuck on Central. I'm not used to driving this far south and the traffic is worse than I thought it would be. If I'd known, I would've left a whole lot earlier."

Franco started to agree, but she heard the same edge of fear in Jenna's voice as she'd heard in Devon's, and she decided to let it go. Jenna was likely more scared than she'd ever been, thinking about her only child facing the prospect of prison. Franco shifted the phone to her other hand and reached for the door to the courtroom. "I'm going back into the courtroom now, so I have to hang up. Get here as soon as you can, but don't break any laws doing it. I'm turning my phone on silent, but I'll watch for a text from you to let me know you're here."

She clicked off the line and looked up in time to see a woman standing in the well of the courtroom. Franco stood rooted in place, simultaneously unable to look away and wishing she could melt into the floor, certain the woman standing across the room was Nina Aguilar. Franco's brain buzzed as she tried to remember the last time she'd seen her. Memories flew, each one specific and detailed, but none of them were recounted in the end. Why couldn't she visualize their good-bye?

A second later, Nina looked up and locked eyes with her. Time and distance fell away and for a brief second, it was like nothing had come between them.

Boom.

Franco saw Nina turn her head at the exact moment she did. She swiveled to the left and back to the right, seeking the source of the noise, but the room started to fill with smoke, impeding her search. What was happening?

❖

Nina tore her gaze from the woman who looked exactly like Franco Rossi and frantically looked for the source of the sound. Something that loud had to be a bomb, but the walls were still standing and the ceiling held. Why were there so many screams and when had the room filled with a thick haze that smelled of fireworks?

As if in answer to her thoughts, the sharp staccato of rapid gunfire erupted into the room, filling it with more smoke and driving the screams to sound louder and more desperate. She whirled in place, seeking the shooter and Lennox and Wren, but she couldn't get her bearings for the fast, furious footfalls, slapping feverishly against the floor all around her. Taking their cue, she ran toward the jury box and squatted behind the short wood barrier, using the vantage point to assess the situation.

She looked toward the spot she'd seen Lennox and Wren, but they weren't there, and she prayed they'd managed to get out in time, because the idea of either one of them being harmed was too much for her to digest. Instinct spurred her to look back across the room for the familiar face, but the woman was gone. If she'd ever even been there at all.

Before she could digest the thought, the haze cleared, and the masked shooter emerged from the cloud of smoke and into the well of the courtroom—determined and dangerous. She ducked lower, but peered around the corner of the box and watched him swing his rifle toward defense counsel table where Devon Grant cowered, especially vulnerable due to the cuffs on his wrists and ankles. The next few moments played out in fuzzy, slow motion. The loud crack of the rifle shot. The blur of a body dashing by her. Nina squinted, certain her eyes were deceiving her, but there was no mistaking that the tall, suited woman diving toward Grant was Franco.

She jumped to her feet and started running, but after a couple of steps she wasn't any closer. The gunman turned and the barrel of the rifle was close. So close, but his eyes were focused on something behind her. She whirled and saw Marty grasping her arm. She opened her mouth to speak, but before she could find words, he shoved her to the ground, and as she fell, a bright red design blossomed across his chest before he slipped to the floor beside her.

She rolled toward him and grabbed his hand. "Marty, are you okay?" She whispered the words and then wondered if he could hear her over the noise of people shouting.

"He ran that way."

"Call 911."

"Is anyone else hurt?"

She forced herself to stay focused on Marty and started to speak again, when someone clasped her shoulder from behind. She whirled toward the touch and gasped at the sight of the familiar face. "Franco?"

"Nina, come on. We have to get out of here."

"Marty's hurt." She pointed at him to prove her point, not caring that Franco would have no idea who Marty was. "What's happening?"

"The shooter took off, but he could come back any minute." Franco bent down and felt Marty's pulse. "It's weak, but he's still alive."

Nina kept her hand pressed on Marty's chest while she

surveyed the wreckage of the still-hazy room. She pointed toward defense counsel table, but Grant was nowhere in sight.

"He's okay. I shoved him into the first row of the gallery," Franco said, reading her mind like she always had.

Nina closed her eyes for a moment. Surely this entire episode wasn't happening. A shooter in her courtroom. An old lover charging in and saving the life of a boy she'd never met, and then comforting her like no time or tribulation had ever passed between them. Her throat closed and suddenly she was desperate to be somewhere else. Anywhere, but here. "I'm going for help."

Franco stood in a quick, seamless motion. "You stay. I'll go."

"And who are you?" Lennox asked.

Nina watched a flash of indignation flash across Franco's face before she turned toward Lennox, who wore a scowl of her own. Nina reached for Lennox's arm, beyond relieved to see her alive, but eager to defuse the situation. "She's an old acquaintance," she said. "Do you mind if we get some help and then discuss my past?"

"I've already called 911 and I imagine everyone in this building is on high alert," Lennox called out toward Franco's back as she walked through the doors toward the hallway. "Whoever that was isn't going to make it out of here."

Nina pulled off her jacket and knelt back by Marty's side, pressing the cloth against his wound, and willing the ambulance to show up soon. "Where's Wren?"

"In your office," Lennox said. "I made her promise to stay there until we got the all clear."

Nina pointed over her shoulder. "Not sure she got the memo on that."

Wren ran toward them. "Oh my God. Is Marty okay? Was anyone else hurt?"

Nina kept her hand on Marty's chest while she swiveled her neck and looked around the room. She spotted two other people lying on the floor between the rows of the gallery. She jerked her chin at Wren, who ran over to them. A moment later, Franco burst back into the room and walked briskly toward her. "What is it?" she asked, certain, by her intense look, that Franco had news. "Did they get him?"

"The shooter's gone. Every law enforcement officer in this building is tuned to a wide-open channel of clusterfuck, and in the confusion, they think he got away." Franco reached down and placed two fingers on Marty's neck. "His pulse is still thready. Ambulances are on the way. If we can move him without causing him too much pain, it would be good to get him downstairs so he can be on the first one."

Nina was torn between feeling like she should maintain order here at the courthouse or accompany Marty to the hospital, and she found herself staring into Franco's eyes like she was some oracle who'd showed up offering guidance during this freak tragedy.

"I'll go," Lennox said.

Nina tore her eyes from Franco's deep gaze and turned toward Lennox. "Thank you. I need to talk to the sheriff and find out what's going on. Text me when you know where they're taking him."

"I will." Lennox helped her to her feet and pulled her into a hug. "Be careful."

As Lennox released the embrace, she gave Franco a withering stare. Nina's first instinct was to tell Lennox to stand down, that Franco was harmless, and staying behind with her was a good thing, but she wasn't sure either of those things were true. All she knew right now was that the former love of her life had chosen a hell of a day to reappear, and as soon as this situation was under control, she was going to find out why.

CHAPTER FOUR

I can't take the case."

Franco stood in Jenna's doorway, her arms folded against her chest to signal the subject was closed, fully prepared to deflect any attempts to persuade her to change her mind. She'd driven directly to Jenna's house after she'd finished answering questions for the police at the courthouse, trading the risk of dipping too deep into her past for the expediency of telling her in person she wouldn't be able to help her son. After what she'd been through today, whatever Jenna had to say wouldn't be enough to convince her to change her mind.

Jenna shivered against the cool night air. "Come in and let's talk about it."

"I'd rather not."

"Well, I'm freezing." Jenna turned to go back inside, leaving the door open behind her. As she walked back into the house, she kept talking. "I get you're having second thoughts. After everything that went down at the courthouse, I'd have second thoughts too, but that had nothing to do with Devon. He needs you, and you haven't even had a chance to hear his side of the story."

Franco stared at Jenna's back for a moment before shaking her head and following her inside. "You have no idea what it was like."

Jenna stopped at the edge of the living room and motioned to a couple of oversized, stuffed chairs before taking a seat. "You're right." She shuddered. "I can't even imagine. If I hadn't hit the traffic jam on Central, I would've been right there in the thick of it. Two people died."

"I know. I was there, remember?" Anger choked her words as she paced the carpet in front of Jenna. "Devon could've been killed."

"And he probably would have if it weren't for you. He called me about an hour ago to let me know what happened and he told me what you did." Jenna reached for her hand. "Please sit down. I promise I won't make you stay."

Franco looked down at her hand in Jenna's. There had been a time when she and Jenna and Nina were inseparable, and while Jenna had always been more Nina's friend than hers, she'd thought they'd always be in each other's lives. But soon after trouble struck, Jenna had ghosted her. She replayed Jenna's comment about how Nina had refused to take her call when Devon had been arrested and wondered what had fractured their friendship.

She settled into the chair across from Jenna's and leaned back against the cushions, letting out her breath in a long, slow release. She wanted to know what had happened to cool Nina and Jenna's relationship, but not enough to ask directly, so she settled on offering up an opening to let Jenna tell her more. "Nina's bailiff is in surgery as we speak. She's pretty worried about him."

"I heard about that on the news." Jenna ducked her head. "I knew she was a judge, but she wasn't assigned to Devon's case. Devon said the bailiff told him the other judge is out on leave."

Her tone was sincere, but too much time had passed for Franco to trust her instincts when it came to people from her past. "Are you absolutely sure about that, because it kind of felt like I was walking into an ambush today, and I'm not talking about the shooter."

"Absolutely not." Jenna shook her head vigorously. "I know you have no reason to trust me after all these years, but I love my son and I wouldn't have put him in the position of having an attorney who suspected I'd tricked her into taking his case."

Exactly what someone would say if they didn't want to risk pissing off the person they'd asked to help them. Franco had spent years honing her internal truth detector, but every once in a while, someone was able to elude her skill. Was that what was happening here or was her past connection to Jenna throwing off her radar? She wasn't sure it mattered either way.

"I know you loved her."

Loved her. Franco pondered the past tense for a moment, but she didn't correct her. Seeing Nina today had brought back a rush of feelings, but she hadn't had time to explore whether they were all dredged from the past or lingering in the present. She wasn't sure she wanted to. She made a snap decision. "I'll help you find someone else to represent Devon. Someone good."

"They won't be as good as you." Jenna waited until they shared eye contact again. "I've done my research. There's no one better than you even if I could get someone local to go up against Harry Benton's influence. And now that I know Nina is the judge on his case, it's even more important that Devon have the best on his side, and who better than someone she always respected."

Respected. Past tense for sure. "What happened between you two?" The question tumbled out of Franco's mouth before she could stop it, but now that it had, she was curious about the answer.

Jenna shook her head. "It's not important. We went our separate ways and I haven't spoken to her in years."

"Sounds like it's more than that."

"It might be, but it's not important to Devon's case."

Franco grew agitated at her evasiveness. "And I'm your secret weapon? The Nina I remember doesn't have a biased bone in her body, but if she did, having me as Devon's attorney would only be a problem, not a solution."

"Maybe. Or maybe she'd bend over backwards to be fair to Devon rather than let anyone think your presence affected her ability to be fair. Let's think this through."

That did it. She'd come to Dallas as a favor to an old friend, but her charity didn't extend to dredging up a painful past and reliving it in open court for all the world to see. It was time to get back to the life she'd created for herself in Houston. "You'll have to think it through with someone else. I'm headed back to Houston." To illustrate her point, she walked toward the door. "I'll send you some names."

Jenna called out to her as she left, but she forced herself to ignore the pleas. She'd crash at her hotel, check on her dad in the morning, and be on the road to Houston before lunchtime.

It was dusk by the time she reached her hotel. Alone in her room, she scanned the room service menu, but the words on the paper blurred as her ability to focus was waylaid by memories of the shooting. The noise, the smells, the sounds of people screaming and stampeding out of the courtroom, all of which overwhelmed her completely. She finally set the menu aside and left the room to head downstairs where she found a spot at the bar.

The petite blond bartender slid a cocktail napkin in front of her. "What can I get you?" she asked.

"Macallan. Neat." She hesitated for a moment. "Make it a

double." No sense holding back since her bed was in the same building.

The bartender nodded her approval and pulled a bottle from the shelf behind her. With her other hand, she reached for a chunky rocks glass and served up a generous pour and handed it her way. Franco tilted the glass toward her before taking a sip and letting the warm buzz of alcohol blaze a healing path through her stress.

"Celebrating or commiserating?"

"Neither," she responded. "Simply blurring the edges of a rough day."

The bartender nodded again and tapped the bar with her hand. "Enjoy the drink. I'll be right over there if you'd like to talk."

The minute she strode away, Franco felt empty again. Maybe discussing what had happened with a total stranger was the perfect solution, but she didn't even know where to begin. *Hey, I came into town to represent the son of a former friend, and while I was at the courthouse, I found out the judge on his case is the former love of my life. If that wasn't enough, her courtroom was full of people and a guy opened fire on all of us, killing some, and leaving her bailiff hanging on for his life. I ducked out of there as fast as I could and now I'm leaving town rather than have to face her again. How great am I?*

Not great at all. Kind of a jerk, actually.

Hell, she didn't need a stranger to have a conversation. She could have one all on her own, arguing both sides. Out in the world, her ability to debate all angles was a skill that commanded big bucks, but in her personal life, it only fractured her focus and annoyed whoever happened to be with her at the time.

She glanced down at her glass and wondered how long it

had been empty since she didn't remember taking the first sip. She raised her arm to signal the bartender, anxious to numb her thoughts until she was ready to stumble back to her room. The bartender nodded in her direction at the exact same moment as a breaking news alert trumpeted from the big TV screen to the right of the bar.

"New developments in this morning's shoot-out at the courthouse. Veteran sheriff's deputy Marty Lafferty has been in surgery for the last seven hours as doctors at Parkland are working furiously to repair multiple gunshot wounds he received during a mass casualty shooting at the courthouse today. Witnesses reported Lafferty rushing people to safety inside the holdover where inmates are kept while they wait to be brought into the courtroom, before he saved the life of Judge Nina Aguilar by coming between her and the gunman's fire. Two other victims of the shooter were pronounced dead at the scene. The shooting took place in Judge Aguilar's courtroom this morning just as proceedings on several notable cases were about to begin. Law enforcement personnel are still questioning witnesses as we speak, but as of right now, the shooter has not been apprehended and is considered armed and dangerous."

"Shit."

"You know that guy? The bailiff?"

Franco tore her gaze from the screen to the bartender, who was watching the TV as well. The bailiff's injuries were worse than she'd noticed when she'd seen him lying in the well of the courtroom. She recalled Nina's obvious distress at Marty's injuries, and she knew exactly where she'd be right now. "I know his boss. She was…" Franco floundered for the right word to describe what Nina had been to her before ultimately deciding it wouldn't matter to this stranger. "She was my friend."

The bartender nodded slowly before reaching for the bottle of Macallan.

Franco held up her hand. "You know what? I changed my mind." She looked at her phone. "Did they say the sheriff's deputy was at Parkland?"

"They did." The bartender cocked her head. "Why? You headed down there?"

Was she? And what would she do when she showed up? Would Nina even talk to her? She had no idea, and thinking about it only made it seem like a silly and impetuous move.

Screw it. "Yes." She stared at her empty glass and decided against driving. "I better get a ride. Any advice for the quickest way to get there?"

"Pal of mine is a Lyft driver, and she hangs out in this area. Head out front and tell the bellman you're waiting on Jackie." She shooed Franco away. "Go, I'll order the car."

Franco slid off the barstool and stood in place for a second before taking off toward the door. Seeing Nina at the courthouse during an adrenaline-boosting shoot-out was one thing but showing up at the hospital was taking things to the next level. They'd shared a moment during the tragedy, but no more than would happen between strangers dealing with the aftermath of a life-changing event, and it was not a gleeful reunion. Still, she needed to show up and offer her support if only to close this chapter of her life once and for all.

When she put it like that, showing up at the hospital sounded perfectly rational. Yeah, right.

CHAPTER FIVE

I brought you some coffee."

Nina looked up to see Wren Bishop standing next to her with two steaming paper cups in her hands. She didn't want any more coffee, but holding the cup would give her something to do with her hands, some semblance of normal, and she needed that more than anything right now. Besides, it was warm, and the hospital was a deep freeze. "Thank you."

Wren pointed to the seat next to her. "You want some company?"

Nina nodded even though the idea she needed company was kind of silly since the room was crowded with personnel from the sheriff's office, all waiting for word of Marty's condition. But unlike everyone else in the room who was focused on Marty and his family, she sensed Wren was there just for her. "Did Lennox tell you to look after me?"

"Maybe." Wren settled into the adjacent chair. "Or maybe I just thought you could use a friend right now. Someone who would get what you're going through because they were there." Wren glanced at the double doors to the surgical floor. "I mean, I didn't know Marty all that well, but he was always very nice to me, especially when I just started out."

Nina smiled at the assessment. Wren had started at the public defender's office last spring as a lawyer on loan from one of the more prominent private law firms in Dallas, but she'd eventually quit her lucrative private practice job to focus on her work representing indigent clients, which also allowed her to work in close proximity to Lennox, though they often wound up on opposite sides of an issue.

"Marty is always nice to the new folks," she said. "He likes to tease me about my first day when I accidentally locked myself out of the door that leads to the bench. He calmly unlocked the door and explained things would get easier with every passing day."

"Such a simple piece of advice, but one hundred percent true, right?"

"Right." She turned in her seat at the sound of the door opening, expecting to see another harried doctor or nurse with their hourly report, but the person standing in front of her was dressed in an expensive suit, not scrubs. "Franco?"

That made twice today she'd said Franco's name with a question mark at the end, but it was impossible to believe she was seeing her old lover in real life, standing only a few feet away after years had passed with complete silence and separation. She'd seen glimpses of her, but never in person— only in the pages of magazine profiles. She was as gorgeous now as she had been the last time she'd seen her. More so.

"Hi, Nina. I hope it's okay I came." Franco nodded at Wren. "Sorry if I'm interrupting."

Nina introduced Wren, who obligingly made an excuse about checking with Marty's doctors and slipped away. She pointed to the now empty chair beside her. "Join me?" Why was she ending every sentence with a question mark?

"Thanks." Franco slid into the chair and crossed her legs. "How is he? They said on the news he's been in surgery for seven hours."

"Eight now, but I'm told that's normal for injuries like this. Apparently, he'd already taken a hit before he took the one meant for me." Nina shook her head, wracked with guilt. "I can't believe he collapsed right in front of me."

Franco shifted in her chair, and for a second, Nina thought she was going to reach for her hand, but at the last second, she crossed her hands in her lap.

"The guy's a freaking hero. Anyone else you know injured?"

"One of the attorneys who died, and Judge Larabee's coordinator, Reggie Knoll, was shot in the shoulder. She was stopping by to drop off some paperwork. Talk about being in the wrong place at the wrong time."

"Tell me about it."

Nina stared hard, unable to fully process what bothered her about what Franco had just said. When her brain finally settled on the thought, she blurted it out before she could mull it over. "Speaking of being in the wrong place at the wrong time, what were you doing at the courthouse today?"

Franco's smile had a slight edge to it. "Well, I *am* a lawyer."

"I can tell by the way you're hedging to avoid answering the question." Nina offered her own smile to soften the remark. "I have to admit I thought I was seeing things when I spotted you right before the shooting started. I thought you were still in Houston." Nina immediately regretted the admission she'd been following Franco's career, but Franco seemed unfazed.

"I was approached to consider a case up here, and this was my first appearance. Case was in Judge Larabee's court, but it appears it was reassigned to you."

Nina mentally skimmed the docket, but it was a bit of a blur. After having had gunfire erupt in her courtroom today, she wasn't sure she could be trusted to recall much of anything, except she'd had a packed schedule. "Did you decide to take the case?"

"I decided against it." Franco didn't meet her eyes. "Some cases aren't the right fit, and this is one of them."

Something about the comment rang familiar, and not in a good way. "You always were quick to walk away from difficult situations."

Franco sat back, like the words had delivered a physical blow, but her eyes were locked on hers with a hard stare. "That's not how I remember it."

"I have no doubt." Nina started to say more but held back. All these years, she'd assumed her anger toward Franco had dissipated, faded along with the memories of what had been and expectations of what could be, but apparently, it had merely lurked just below the surface. Or maybe she was simply on edge from the shooting. Whatever it was, sitting next to Franco Rossi right now and pretending their past wasn't fraught with pitfalls, was beyond her. "I'm sorry for what I said, but I meant it."

Franco choked out a laugh. "Which is a backhanded way of saying you're not sorry."

"I guess you're right." No sense trying to deny it. "Would you believe me if I also said I'm sorry I can't get past it?"

Franco didn't break eye contact. "Yes. Would you believe me if I said I'm sorry too?" She stood without waiting for an answer. "I should go. I'm sorry for busting in, but I wanted to make sure you were okay. And that Marty is okay."

Nina didn't bother pointing out that there were many ways Franco could've found out the same information without showing up at the hospital, but that would invite an explanation and she wasn't certain she wanted to know why Franco had felt the need to show up in person. Well, that wasn't accurate. She really did want to know, but she knew that hearing the answer might change her life somehow and she wasn't at all prepared for a seismic shift and whatever fallout came with it. Not right now. Not while Marty was open on a table, fighting for his life and not while she was still processing her own feelings about the shootout in her courtroom. "Have a safe trip home."

"Thanks."

Franco lingered, even opened her mouth as if she had more to say, but no words came out, and after a few awkward moments of silence, she turned and walked to the door. Before she reached it, two doctors dressed in scrubs burst into the room. A hush fell over the crowd, and Nina leaned against the now empty chair next to her and started to stand, because judging by the expression on their faces, this visit wasn't a simple interim update. She pushed against the metal arm of the chair for support, but a soft grip on her arm was the real steadying force. She glanced over to see Franco standing back at her side, delivering a gentle and encouraging smile. She wanted to melt into the familiarity she'd long forgotten, but she also wanted to run away from it at the same time.

She shook her head. It was too much to process. She turned back to the doctors and held her breath while she waited for them to deliver the news. The tall woman in the unicorn scrub cap spoke first.

"He suffered severe injuries, but we've made all the necessary repairs and if all goes well in the next twenty-four hours, he should recover without any permanent damage." She paused and looked around the room as if taking in the weight of how many supporters were hanging on her every word. "He's going to be in recovery for several hours and in the ICU after that. Immediate family members only can visit, and then only one at a time. I know you all probably want to see him, but the best way for you to do that is to let him heal so he sticks around for the long term. Trust me, he's going to be happier to see your faces when he's not wearing a gown that ties in the back."

The crowd, grateful for the jolt of levity, responded with laughter. Nina breathed a sigh of relief, and with it, the last dregs of adrenaline that had fueled her resolve ebbed and exhaustion swept through her.

"Are you okay?"

Franco's husky whisper and soft breath against her ear stripped away the tired, and she struggled to focus against the onslaught of feelings the simple gesture evoked. "I'm good, but I think I should go." She took a step away from Franco, away from the temptation of her tenderness, telling herself it was nothing more than sympathy. She faltered on the second step and gripped the back of the chair next to her, again feeling the secure grip of Franco's hand on her arm.

"You're exhausted. How did you get here? Did you drive your own car?"

Why were they talking about transportation? Nina's eyelids were feeling very heavy and visions of crisp, cool bedsheets and a mountain of pillows filled her thoughts. "I don't remember. Maybe I got a ride."

"I'll take you home."

Nina watched Franco punch some buttons on her phone. Who was she calling? Her thoughts swam. Franco must be really busy to have to interact with people this late in the day. Well, of course she was busy. She was a good attorney. A great one, if you believed all the accolades she'd received. But as busy as she was, right now she was here at the hospital, looking after her.

"The car will be here in five minutes." Franco extended her arm. "Let's head downstairs."

"Where are you going?"

Nina recognized Lennox's voice and the slight edge beneath the words. She turned to face her friend and pulled her into a fierce hug. "Where have you been? Did they question you all this time?"

Lennox hugged her back, but Nina could feel the tension in her body, and when they broke their embrace, she saw Lennox was still staring at Franco.

"There was a lot to debrief," Lennox said. "They had a lot of questions about everyone who had a case set in your courtroom today." She gave Franco a hard look. "Especially people who weren't expected."

Nina saw Franco raise her eyebrows, but thankfully, she didn't engage with Lennox. "I'm sure that's standard practice, and they'll want to talk to me as well."

"They'll hold off until tomorrow. I explained you were here and not to be disturbed." Another pointed glance at Franco, who'd stepped off to the side, ostensibly to give them some privacy.

"She's a friend," Nina whispered.

"She looks at you like it's more than that."

Nina rolled her eyes. "It's not. And I don't need protecting. I'm going home now, but I'll talk to you in the morning. You should get Wren and go home too. Tonight, everyone should hold the ones they love close."

Lennox's expression softened and she pulled Nina into a tight hug. "Good plan. Call me if you need me. Okay?"

"I will." Nina watched her walk away before turning back to Franco, who looked like she was pretending not to watch their every move. She had one last opportunity to close the door on her past, and she hesitated for a moment. Her feelings were jumbled and messy and raw, but she wasn't entirely sure whether the source of her angst was related to seeing Franco after such a long time or the experience of having her courtroom become a crime scene. Whatever it was, curiosity about what Franco had been doing with her life all these years was strong enough to lower—slightly—the wall she'd put in place years ago. "I'm ready to go now."

"Good. The car just pulled up."

Her advice to Lennox played on a loop in her head as they rode the elevator to the lobby. She'd spent her entire adult life looking for a love like the one she'd had with Franco, only to come up empty at every turn. How ironic that Franco had come back into her life on the very day she could use someone the most. Now she needed to figure out what to do with that information and keep herself safe from being hurt by her again.

CHAPTER SIX

Franco glanced over at Nina, who sat in the back seat of the Lyft with her eyes closed and her head resting against the window. So far, the ride to Nina's house had been mostly silent and the only one attempting conversation was Jackie, the same driver who'd transported her from the hotel to the hospital. Nina's reticence to talk made Franco question whether choosing to check in on her had been a good idea. Clearly, Nina had other people in her life, including the fierce prosecutor who appeared to have a jealous streak. Well, if Lennox Roy wanted to look out for Nina, she should've been at the hospital with her from the get-go, making sure she was okay.

Nina isn't yours to look out for anymore. Besides, you're the one who walked away.

The voice in her head spoke the truth, but the urge to step up today was out of her control. It had been years since she'd seen Nina, but standing across the courtroom from her, all the old feelings lurched back into life, like zombies woken from the dead. Clumsy and awkward, but focused on a singular mission. That had to change. Rekindling their long dead romance was a nonstarter, but maybe, just maybe, they could find a way to move past the pain of their past and have a friendship of sorts, or at least be cordial.

When Jackie pulled up to a small Tudor home in East Dallas, Franco looked over at Nina, who was now slumped against the window and sound asleep. Franco stared at her for a moment, contemplating what to do next. Clearly, she hadn't thought this through.

"Everything okay?" Jackie asked.

The words shook Franco out of her trance. "I should make sure she gets inside okay."

"I'll wait for you. Do you need help?"

"No," Franco said as she slipped her arm around Nina's shoulders. "I'm good." She paused for a moment. Torn about whether to accept Jackie's offer. "And you don't have to stay. Really."

There. She'd committed to getting Nina settled and that was okay, right?

Jackie shot her a knowing smile and handed her a card. "That's my number. If you need me later. For a ride or whatever. I'll be working in the morning if it's that kind of a night."

Franco accepted the card because it was the polite thing to do, but she didn't bother trying to correct Jackie's assumption that she planned to spend the night with Nina. She tucked it into her jacket pocket and focused on helping the now awake Nina out of the car. Once the cool night air hit them both, Nina seemed to perk up and walk just fine, but she leaned into Franco's embrace in a way that felt strange and familiar at the same time, and Franco held her close as if nothing had ever come between them.

When they reached the front door, Nina pulled her keys out of her purse, but they shook in her hand. "Here, let me," Franco said, reaching for them, trying and failing to ignore the current of sensation that came from touching Nina's hand. She should've told Jackie to stick around because suddenly she was consumed with the desire to flee this place, this woman. She'd had no business coming back to Dallas. All the good memories were tainted by the mistakes she'd made here, and no amount of time and space would change the past. She stuck the key in the lock and it turned smoothly, providing easy access. If only their relationship could be so easy. But it couldn't. She'd see Nina safely inside and then get the hell out. She pushed open the door to a high-pitched tone that blared into the night.

"The alarm," Nina said, moving quickly to punch numbers into the keypad on the wall.

The warmth that whooshed away when Nina stepped out of her embrace stole Franco's breath, but she recovered enough to say, "I should go."

"Please don't. I haven't seen you in years, and this day… Well, I don't even know what to say about this day except it still feels so surreal. Does it feel that way to you? How about a drink? I need a whisky. You?"

The blur of questions caught her off guard and Franco stared at the door as if it would tell her what to do next. Nina's hand on her arm was the deciding factor.

"Take off your jacket and come with me to the kitchen."

She complied like it was the most natural thing to do. Nina's kitchen was enormous, bright, and beautiful—the kind she'd always said she wanted, and Franco was instantly transported back in time.

"One day, I'm going to have a kitchen the size of this apartment."

"That's a pretty big kitchen," Franco said. "You giving up your dream of being a legal eagle to compete on Top Chef*?"*

"Maybe. Or maybe I just want a place where friends and family feel comfortable hanging out, sharing a meal, talking

and drinking. Not like my parents' house where everything is so...perfect. You know, a place where everyone is comfortable— like it's their own home."

"So, all the big holiday gatherings will be at our place."

"You okay with that?"

Franco grinned. "I'm okay with anything that involves you, me, and our future."

"Good." Nina tucked her arms through Franco's and pulled her close. "Because I have a lot of other plans, and they all involve you."

"Is this okay?"

Franco looked up to see Nina holding a short, chunky glass half full of amber liquid. None of Nina's plans had come to fruition, not for the two of them anyway, but she'd gotten her kitchen. Was there someone else who she planned to share it with? She took the glass and sipped the whisky, a smooth, smoky Scotch, that immediately took the edge off the day.

"Do you live here by yourself?"

"You never were one to beat around the bush."

"And you never used to duck questions."

Nina flicked her gaze away. "A lot's changed since freshman year of college. But to answer your question, I live here alone. I haven't met someone I'd like to share my kitchen with yet."

"It's everything I imagined when you used to talk about it. You should definitely hold out for the right person to share it with."

Nina stared into her eyes for a moment and then pointed back toward the front of the house. "I need to sit. Will you sit with me for a bit?"

"Of course."

Franco followed her back into the living room and,

following her lead, took a seat in one of the club chairs near the fireplace. Nina sank into the couch, toed off her shoes, and swung her legs onto the cushions. She, on the other hand, sat on the end of her chair, her body and mind on high alert against the influx of memories and the flood of accompanying feelings. They sat in silence for a while, each sipping from their drink like the quiet between them was companionable, but Franco feared it was only a prelude to an explosion.

Finally, unable to stand the quiet, she spoke first. "I should've reached out before now."

"Yes. Yes, you should've."

She wasn't sure what she expected, but Nina's declaration was fair. "I didn't think you'd want to hear from me."

"I didn't. Not for a very long time, but we're past all that nonsense now. We've moved on with our lives. Maybe an apology would've gone a long way to healing. For both of us."

Franco shifted in her seat. "I think we're beyond that now."

"After all this time, I recognize that's your way of saying I should let it go. Things don't always work that way."

"Maybe they should."

"Is that why you never got in touch? Because after you abruptly tossed me out of your life, you thought things would miraculously shift back to normal at some point without you having to put any effort into making it so?" Nina set her glass of wine down and crossed her arms. "Even someone as arrogant as you must realize not everything magically resolves itself simply because you will it to."

"Did you just call me arrogant?" Franco wasn't sure she wanted to hear Nina confirm what they both knew she'd said, but she could hardly believe Nina held such a low opinion of her after all this time.

"What word would you use?"

"I made a mistake. I thought I was doing the right thing at the time. We were young. Young people make mistakes."

"My only mistake was thinking you wouldn't toss me to the side when things got rough. You cut me out of your life and I have no idea why. It's like you didn't trust me to stand by you no matter what, and as a consequence you let us both down."

The pain in Nina's voice penetrated deep. She supposed she shouldn't be surprised. While she knew they'd never be able to recapture the love they'd shared, she'd led herself to believe that one day when they encountered each other again, they would be able to see beyond the past and find a place deeper than cordial. But barely friendly was apparently all she could hope for. "I'm not the same person I used to be. I expect you aren't either."

"Does it matter? If I learned anything today, it's that life is only what you have in the moment. Our moment is long gone." Nina stood. "If you're seeking some blessing from me, some assurance that all is well, I can't give you what you're looking for. Go home, Franco."

At the door, Franco turned and stared into Nina's eyes one last time. "I never meant to hurt you. It's important that you know that."

"Careless pain slices as deep as the cuts you intend to inflict. Go home, Franco."

Franco waited until the door was shut and she heard Nina's footsteps fade before she summoned Jackie on her phone, but Nina's voice echoed in her head. Home had so many different meanings, and the first place that came to mind wasn't her palatial apartment in Houston, but a place much closer. Time to make one more stop on the train to her past before reentering her present.

CHAPTER SEVEN

Nina stood outside the double doors of her courtroom. The hall was teeming with crowds of people—defendants, attorneys, jurors—all of them going about their business as if a shooting hadn't happened mere yards away only days ago. But Marty was still in the hospital, and his blood along with the other victims of the shooting still stained the carpet across the hall. The memory of last Friday would be slow to fade.

"Good morning, Judge."

She glanced to her left to see Reggie Knoll, Judge Larabee's court coordinator, standing next to her and staring at the doors. "Good morning." She gestured at the sling around her neck. "How's your shoulder?"

Reggie grimaced. "I'm not going to lie. It's pretty painful."

Nina felt a quick stab of guilt that she'd escaped the shooting unscathed. "You don't have to be back here so soon. No one would think any less of you if you took some time off."

"I'd think less of me. And I think it might be a little like falling off a horse. Best thing to do is jump right back in."

Nina heard past the brave words and caught an edge of fear, but she knew she'd probably feel exactly the same. This was her domain and if a shooter thought they were going to take it from her, they were sorely mistaken.

"We're all set up for you over here." Reggie motioned to

another set of doors over to the left. "Come on, I'll walk you through today's docket."

As if in a trance, Nina followed Reggie past the court clerk's office, down a hallway to a suite of offices, one for Reggie; one for the court reporter, William; and finally, Judge Larabee's chambers, where she'd be working until the police department finished gathering evidence in her own courtroom.

"Are you okay, Judge?"

Nina snapped to attention when she realized they were still standing in the doorway to Judge Larabee's chambers. She needed to pull it together if she was going to make it through her first day back, but she also wanted answers about what had happened, or she'd never be able to get past the dread she'd felt when she'd walked through the doors of the building this morning. She pointed at the door. "Come inside with me for a sec?"

Once inside Larrabee's office, she sat down behind the desk and Reggie settled into one of the chairs across from her. Nina folded her hands on the desktop and took a deep breath. "I have a lot of feelings about being back here so soon, and I'm sure you do too."

"Completely senseless and brutal," Reggie said. "But like I said in the hall, I'm ready to be back. If you're here, I'm here."

Nina took a moment to appraise Reggie. She and Larabee often covered for each other and Reggie had always been cordial, but she didn't know her all that well. Lennox had gone out with her a few times before she'd met Wren, and said she was nice, but the chemistry wasn't there. That about summed up all she knew about her temporary coordinator, but the fact she was here and ready to work after being shot less than a week ago gave her a healthy amount of respect for the woman. "Before we get started on the docket, I have a favor to ask."

"Name it."

"The police department is investigating the shooter. You close with any DPD officers?"

"A few. There are some regulars who wind up down here as witnesses. We talk."

"Great. Mind talking to them and seeing what you can find out about the investigation? I'm not trying to influence anything, but I don't want to be shielded from it either."

"It happened in your courtroom—you have a right to know."

"Exactly."

Reggie nodded. "I can respect that. I'll see what I can find out and report back, good or bad."

"Thank you. Now, tell me what we've got lined up for today."

They spent the next fifteen minutes going through the list of pending cases and a few motions that were waiting on pro forma rulings. When they finished up, Nina put on her black robe and slowly walked out of her office and back down the hall to the door that led to the bench. Her breathing grew shallow as she put her hand on the doorknob. It wasn't her door, it wasn't her bench, but it was similar enough to evoke an undeniable sense of dread. *If I don't do this now, it's only going to get harder.* She repeated the mantra on a loop in her head, until she was finally able to turn the knob and climb the few steps to sit behind the bench.

The courtroom was bustling as usual for a Monday morning, almost as if a mass shooting hadn't taken place across the hall mere days ago. Life went on was the lesson here, and she decided to embrace that reality and plow forward. She signaled to the bailiff to bring out the first defendant and she called the case.

She was on the third plea when she spotted Lennox enter the courtroom and take a seat in the very back. She suspected she was here to check on her as much as she was checking on the prosecutors under her supervision, and she nodded her way, and then glanced at the clock. When the plea finished up, she called a brief recess and went back to her chambers. As expected, Lennox showed up a few minutes later.

"You okay?" Lennox asked as she walked into the room.

"Yes. Why does everyone ask me that? I mean all of you were here on Friday too. It's not like I'm the only one with a case of PTSD."

"Yes, but 'it' happened in your courtroom. You're displaced now and it has to bring up feelings."

"You've suddenly become the warm and sensitive type?" Nina smiled to soften her words. "Your girlfriend is rubbing off on you."

"Is that a bad thing?"

"Not in the least, but seriously, you don't have to worry about me. I'm fine. Coming right back to work was probably the best thing I could've done."

"You want to tell me about the woman you left with Friday night?"

She'd known she'd have to explain at some point and maybe it was best to do it with attorneys in the courtroom waiting on her, so she'd have an excuse to bail on the conversation as quickly as possible. "Blast from the past."

"How far back?"

Nina sighed. "Way back. High school. College."

"Friend?"

"Lover." Nina was surprised at how easily the word rolled

off her tongue considering how many years it had been since she'd thought of Franco that way.

"Ye, you've never mentioned her."

"It was almost twenty years ago. Long before I met you, and there's nothing to mention. I haven't seen her since we were freshmen in college, and we haven't kept in touch."

"What's she doing here?"

Nina shifted in her seat. On a normal day, she was used to Lennox's tendency to drill down on a subject, but most of the time she wasn't the object of the interrogation. She knew not answering would only heighten Lennox's curiosity about all things Franco Rossi, but she could be as vague as possible. "Not clear. She's a lawyer and she was here checking out a case. She gave me a ride home Friday and then took off. She lives in Houston, I think. I'll probably never see her again."

Nina gathered her files and stood. "In the meantime, there are a bunch of other lawyers in the courtroom waiting on yours truly, so I better get going."

Lennox cocked her head like she was about to ask more questions, but then shrugged. "Fine. We'll talk later. You're still coming over to our place next weekend, right? We're kind of counting on you to make the margaritas."

"Like I'm going to let anyone else get between me and the tequila. You're on." She play-punched Lennox on the shoulder. "Look at you. A new promotion and a new house. You're living your best life right now."

"It was quick, I know, but it's a great house and we didn't want to risk losing it."

"I can't wait to see it." Nina narrowed her eyes. "You look really happy."

A touch of pink appeared on Lennox's cheeks. "Courtroom shooting aside, things are pretty good right now."

Nina pulled her into a hug. "You deserve all the good things."

"I don't know about that, but I'm making the most of it. Still, I think about Daniel sitting in prison and I don't feel right celebrating anything until I get to the bottom of what went down with his plea."

Nina nodded. Lennox's brother had plead guilty to manslaughter a number of years ago and was doing time at a prison a couple of hours away. Lennox was convinced there was something off about the plea and that there was a chance her brother wasn't guilty since he didn't remember committing the crime. She and Wren were delving further into the details, but so far they hadn't turned up anything that would help them exonerate Daniel. "Let me know if there's anything I can do to help, but in the meantime, you're allowed to celebrate now and then celebrate again when Daniel is free."

Lennox shook a finger at her. "I'll definitely keep that in mind. Now, go be all judgy since that's what the good people of Dallas County elected you to do."

When the door closed behind Lennox, Nina hung back for a moment. She hadn't been entirely honest with Lennox—a first for their friendship, but she wasn't ready to deal with the feeling evoked when she talked about Franco. Or thought about Franco. Or imagined a life with Franco that could've been. Unbidden, a scene played in her head:

"I know you didn't do this. Why won't you let me help you?"

Franco edged out of her embrace. "I did do it and I have to pay the consequences. It's simple, really."

"You could get kicked out of school. And what about our plans to go to law school together? You won't get into Richards with a criminal record."

"Law school is your future, not mine."

"I thought it was a plan we made together."

Franco ducked her head and stared at the ground. "I only said I'd go because I didn't want to disappoint you, but here's the thing. I'll only ever disappoint you. I'm sorry I stole the drugs. It was stupid, but I'm not letting my dad go to prison for it." She looked up and her eyes were ringed with pain. "It's time for us to go our separate ways."

Nina grabbed Franco's hands, determined this wasn't going to be the end for them. "No, we're going to stick together and fight these charges."

"No, we're not. It's my battle to fight, and I'm not interested. Walk away, Nina. It's the best thing for both of us."

Nina wept openly now. "It's not the best thing, Franco. You don't get to decide what's best for me. And when I talk about fighting, I'm not simply talking about fighting the charges against you, I'm talking about fighting for us. This is our battle, and you cannot tell me it's best to let it go."

Franco's faced twisted in pain, but she didn't relent. "It is for the best. You have to trust me. I love you, Nina, and all I want, all I need from you right now is for you to turn around, walk away, and don't look back. If you love me, you'll do it."

"Never."

"Fine, then I'll leave. Live a good life and do all the things you've dreamed of. You're going to be an amazing lawyer."

With those words, Franco had turned and walked away, and until a few days ago, that had been the last time Nina had seen her. She'd thought she was long past feeling anything about it, but that was a lie. Part of her was relieved Franco had left a second time, but another part of her regretted not delving deeper into why they'd ever broken up in the first place.

Maybe you'll have another chance.

CHAPTER EIGHT

M onday morning, Franco rolled out of bed and stretched her arms above her head in an attempt to relieve the ache in her back from sleeping on what she believed was the same mattress she'd had when she was in high school. Judging by the state of the rest of the room, she was probably right. Two Indigo Girls and an Erin Brockovich poster still hung on the wall, and the furniture was the same hand-me-down pieces her parents had given her when they finally splurged on a new set from Sears a few years before she graduated high school. Time had stood still in this place while so much had changed in the outside world.

She dressed in jeans and a T-shirt and wandered into the living room to find her father sleeping in his favorite recliner, which, like her bedroom furniture, was circa 1980. She stood and stared, listening to his light snores, and wondered when his face had filled with wrinkles.

How long had it been since she'd been back to Dallas? In her head it had been around six months, but it might've been a year, maybe longer. However long, he'd aged in the interim—way more than she'd expected, and the realization was disturbing.

She made her way into the kitchen with its dated color

scheme and ancient appliances. Quietly, so as not to wake him, she made coffee and went outside to drink it on the deck they had built together, many years ago. The wood was weathered and rotting in places. Like everything else in the house, it was starved for attention, and she'd started making a list. What was supposed to be a relaxing ritual of coffee outside quickly turned into an anxious assessment of how much needed to be done around here to keep her dad's place from crumbling away, and she decided to get to work.

When she passed back by the recliner, her dad was awake, but just like when she'd shown up at the house Friday night, at first his eyes didn't reflect any recognition at the sight of her. "Hey, Pop, you get a good night's sleep?" she asked, hoping the sound of her voice would spark his memory.

"Good morning, Frances," he said, fumbling for the push arm to the recliner. "Have you eaten? How about I make you some eggs and bacon?"

Her mind flashed to the nearly empty fridge, and she placed her hand on top of his to still his motion. "It's still early. Go back to sleep. We can make breakfast together in a while."

He frowned and for a second, she thought he was going to protest, but then his eyes fluttered shut and the light snores resumed moments later. There was definitely something wrong with him, and she added making a doctor's appointment to her list.

Franco spent the balance of the day tackling the repairs she could with whatever supplies she could find in the garage, making a list of additional items she'd need to purchase as she went. She took a short break at lunch to heat up a can of soup—one of the only unexpired food items she could find—and served it to her dad, before returning to the job while he faded back into another nap. When she'd finished everything she could do with the supplies on hand, she reviewed her supply list, grabbed her keys, and headed for her car. She'd barely made it out the door when her phone rang. She glanced at the display and answered it on the second ring. "Hey, Julie, what's up?"

"Good morning, stranger. Hank Dillard has been calling all morning. He wants to talk to you about the trial date and see if you'll agree to a motion to continue."

It took her a moment to register who Julie was talking about before she remembered that Hank was co-counsel with her on a case that was set for trial next month in federal court. "Did he say why he needs a reset?" she asked, certain she was supposed to remember, but her mind couldn't conjure the details.

"The expert witness he wants to hire is booked through February. The prosecutor doesn't have a problem with it, so it's an agreed motion if you'll sign off."

"Sure, yeah, let's do it." Franco waited a beat while she considered a decision she'd been mulling all morning. "And, Julie?"

"Yes?"

"Tell Trey I'm going to need him to step in on a few matters," she said, referring to her top senior associate "I'm staying in Dallas for a while. I'll be available by phone if you need me, but I've got to take care of a few things for my dad."

"Everything okay?"

She glanced back at the room where Pop was sleeping. "It will be."

"Are *you* okay? Friday was a traumatic day even for those of us who only watched the fallout on the news. I can't even imagine what it must have been like to be there in person."

Franco heard the concern in her voice. She was the first person who'd asked about her following the shooting. She hadn't told Pop she'd been at the courthouse that day—it would only confuse him and make him realize he hadn't been the primary reason she'd come to town, and while that was true, she didn't want to hurt his feelings.

"To be honest, I don't know. I haven't really had a chance to think about it, but it was awful."

"Go easy. You're probably going to experience it in stages."

"Spoken like the wife of a psychiatrist."

"Don't knock the free advice. And stay as long as you need to. Being with family will do you good."

Franco replayed Julie's words after she hung up, questioning their truth. Family was more of an obligation than a comfort, and being back in her childhood home was a reminder of what she'd lost when she'd chosen the family she'd been born into over one she made on her own. She didn't expect anyone else to understand that, and she knew she'd come across as touched to anyone who heard her try to articulate how it felt to be back here.

But here she was, and she'd just committed to stay for a while, no matter what the motivation. She grabbed the list and her keys and let herself out.

She passed a Home Depot about a mile from the house, but she drove on by. There was a time she'd had to settle for whatever you could get at the cheapest store, but she'd earned the right and the income to make better choices. Elliot's Hardware was in the Casa Linda shopping center exactly where she remembered it, and she jockeyed for a parking space close to the door. A stocky Marine-looking guy greeted her at the door and handed her a cart. After asking him a few questions about locating supplies for some of the repairs she had planned, she wheeled the cart into the center of the store and commenced to filling it with the things she needed along with a random assortment of other items. Tiki torches for the back deck, new racks and charcoal for the grill, and a couple of green plants to give the place a semblance of life.

She might not be able to keep her father from aging, but she could make sure he had all the creature comforts while he did. When she finished at the store and loaded everything into the car, she drove through the lot and parked at the grocery store on the far end. She jotted down a few more things on the list she'd made that morning and headed inside. She was halfway through the produce aisle when she spotted Nina standing several feet away holding a bag of grapes. Her first instinct was to duck down the nearest aisle, but before she could make her move, Nina looked up and waved in her direction. She hid a sigh and walked over to her. "Those aren't good for you. Orbs of sugar."

Nina cracked a half smile. "Maybe I'm not interested in what's good for me right now."

"You should be. If you're not going to look out for yourself, who will?"

"Good question." Nina looked her up and down. "I guess you know what you're talking about since it's pretty clear you take excellent care of yourself."

Was Nina flirting with her? It had been such a long time, she wasn't sure if she recalled what her flirting moves looked like, but two could play this game. "Right back at you."

"Did you decide to take the case after all?"

The question caught her off guard. "Case?"

"You were here for a case, but then a gunman opened fire in the courtroom. Help me out here—I can't be the only one who remembers what happened last week."

Right. That. "Sorry. It's been a crazy few days." She paused for a moment while she considered telling her it was Jenna who'd contacted her about the case but decided against it. "I said no to the case."

Nina gave her shopping cart a pointed look. "Buying groceries seems like a funny thing for a person to be doing when they're headed back to their life in another part of the state."

"They're for my dad." She didn't owe Nina an explanation, but she decided it would be easier to offer up a harmless detail.

"Is he okay?"

"He's fine." Franco hesitated for a moment and then blurted out her concerns. "He's not great. Listless, creaky. Not a lot of energy. I need to get him in to see the doctor this week. I have no idea when his last checkup was, but something's wrong."

"So, you're staying."

Franco wasn't sure if she detected hope or disappointment in Nina's tone. "Only long enough to make sure he's okay." She pointed at the cart. "He didn't have a lot on hand. Figured I'd stock him up."

"I see you still like those thumbprint cookies. Those are for you, right?"

Franco bit back a grin, but the familiarity of the memory warmed her. Leave it to Nina to remember the little details and bring them out at just the right moment. "You know they are."

"I guess some things never change."

"I guess that's true." Franco met Nina's eyes and let the gaze linger longer than she'd planned. "And other things change completely."

"True. True." Nina cast a look over her shoulder. "I should get back to it. Have fun shopping and tell your dad I said hello."

"I will," Franco lied. She wasn't interested in hearing him rail at her about how she'd handled things between her and Nina all those years ago. "Take care." She wheeled her cart away before she got lost in the moment, but she was only halfway down the aisle when Nina's voice called out to her again.

"Let me know if you need anything. I can always check in on him if you'd like."

The offer was touching and sweet and Franco planned to never take her up on it, but like everything else from her past, it was best to simply pretend it was okay. "Thanks. I will."

❖

"You saw her in the grocery store?" Lennox asked, looking up from the menu. "I thought she was leaving?"

"Me too, but she's staying in town to take care of her father. There she was, buying produce and cookies and looking gorgeous doing it." Nina grabbed the menu from Lennox's grasp. After spotting Franco at the store, she'd been unable to concentrate on any of the work she'd brought home. She'd called Lennox, who was happy to join her for dinner since Wren was working late. "Pay attention. This is important."

"More important than me deciding how big an order of fries to get?"

"Past love beats French fries, every day of the week."

"Good thing past loves don't pop up that often," Lennox said. "I'm starving."

"Come on, who was there for you when you were falling for Wren?" Nina instantly regretted her choice of words when Lennox set down her menu and fixed her with a hard stare.

"Are you falling for Franco Rossi?"

She wasn't. Not at all, but the question threw her off balance, and she answered quickly to cover how disconcerted it made her. "Key word 'past.'" She waved her arms like she was trying to erase their last exchange. "Besides, you're missing the point. What do you think she's doing here?"

"You said she's taking care of her father."

"But that wasn't why she showed up in Dallas, right? I mean, she was at the courthouse last week." Lennox set the menu down and folded her hands on the table. "I looked her up."

This was the perfect time for Nina to confess she'd done her fair share of googling as well, but she couldn't seem to cough up the confession. Not even to her best friend. "Find anything interesting?"

"A few things, actually. She's been licensed three years less than you. Graduated from Rice. Prosecutor pal of mine in Harris County says most of her clients are either very rich or very poor. She's got a plush office near the Galleria, but she takes cases from the wheel on a regular basis."

Nina nodded and reached for her drink, stalling her response. She'd learned essentially the same information, except the last detail about Franco taking a fair share of court-appointed cases. She wasn't sure what to do with the knowledge, but thankfully, their server showed up to take their order and save her from mustering up a response to Lennox's announcement. She focused on the menu like it was the study guide for the bar exam, finally settling on a burger. She'd been stress eating since the shooting, and with the way this conversation was going, there was no sense stopping now.

As soon as their server left, Lennox launched right back into topic Franco. "She has several associates, but she handles the appointed cases herself. Word is she's honest, but tough. Always ready to go to trial, but practical about when to take a deal."

"Look at you waxing on about a defense attorney," Nina said with a grin. "Guess dating one has made you soft."

"As if. Just reporting what I found out." She put her hands on the table and leaned closer. "There's one more thing."

A chill settled over Nina, and she was certain she knew what Lennox was about to say but held out a small fraction of hope she hadn't been able to unearth Franco's secret. "Spill."

"There's a rumor that she's had her own stint as a defendant." Lennox cocked her head. "Why did you just go pale?"

"I don't know what you're talking about." Nina fixed her face into what she hoped was an expression of sincere surprise.

"All the color drained from your face, and you edged forward in your seat like you're ready to bolt. What's up?"

Nina wanted to make some excuse about being hungry, tired, anything except what was really the matter. But the fact was she couldn't stand letting Lennox keep going on about Franco when she was sitting right in front of her with all the missing details. She'd always been honest with Lennox, even when it was painful, but this was next level, and it really wasn't her story to tell. Or was it?

Damn. "I want to tell you something, but it's private. Not just for me, but for Franco. Promise me you won't say anything to anyone."

Lennox raised an eyebrow. "I'm super curious, but do you mean I can't tell anyone *at all?*"

Nina noted the emphasis and instantly clued into Lennox's real question. "Fine, you can tell Wren, but nobody else. Promise."

Lennox made a show of crossing her heart. "Promise."

"Franco *was* a defendant. She pled no contest to stealing meds from the drugstore where her father worked."

"She stole drugs? Where did he work? Was he a pharmacist? Did he—"

Nina held up a hand to stop the rapid-fire questions. "He

worked in the stockroom at Jenson's Pharmacy, downtown. And she pled no contest in an agreed plea. We were freshman in college and madly in love, but the fallout ended us."

Lennox whistled low. "Wow. So, you broke up in college. Did you know she went to law school?" She frowned. "Wait. How did she get into law school? And Rice of all places? I would've thought they'd have higher standards."

A persistent need to defend Franco bubbled up, but Nina tempered the urge to embrace it full-on and offered a gentle admonishment instead. "Come on, Lennox. You don't have to act like a prosecutor in your off hours."

Lennox patted her jacket pocket where Nina knew she kept her badge. "No acting here. I'm always a prosecutor. You said she pled guilty."

"I said she pled no contest."

"Same thing. Let me guess, the prosecutor had to sign off on the exact wording of the plea. It was part of the deal, right?"

"Why do you care so much?"

"Because this is something big that happened to someone you were in love with and I can tell it affected you. And it's interesting. So, were you in court for the plea or had you already broken up before that?"

"Your interest in the details of the most painful breakup of my life is touching." She stole some fries from Lennox's plate. Not that she was hungry, but it was a way to stall, to focus on something other than the memory of Franco's face the last time they'd spoken.

"I don't understand why you're breaking up with me." Nina was full-on sobbing and certain she was slurring her words. *"It's more important than ever that we have each other for support."*

"No, Nina. I have responsibilities, and they don't include you." Franco turned her face away before she spoke again. "Besides, I'm dropping out. Turns out your parents were right about me all along."

Nina flinched at the memory of Franco walking up during more than one of the "conversations" aka smackdowns her parents had with her to express their disapproval of their relationship. "My parents don't know what's best for me. They never have." She clutched Franco's arm. "But you do. You always have. Please don't walk away from me now."

"I've made my decision." Franco shook her head. "It's done."

Nina ran her hands up Franco's side, lingering over her neck and letting her hands come to rest on either side of Franco's beautiful face. The very idea she'd never see this face again, never wake up to her voice whispering promises of love, of a future, was inconceivable. "It doesn't have to be. I have money of my own. We can hire the best lawyer in the state."

"Money isn't the answer to everything."

"No, but it can open doors. Don't be stubborn, Franco."

Franco reached up and curled her hands around Nina's. "I promise you, this isn't me being stubborn. This is me doing the right thing. Can you trust that I know what I'm doing?"

Nina stared into Franco's eyes for a moment, but it was like Franco had erected a wall and she couldn't figure out a way to get through. "I want to, but I don't understand. Help me understand, Franco. Please help me understand."

Franco gently released her grip on Nina's hands and lowered them to her side. She took a step away. First one, then another, and Nina could feel the whoosh of space widen between them. Franco was walking away—from college, from *her, from their future together. She didn't understand it and Franco wasn't even trying to explain, and now that it was happening, she felt powerless to stop her.*

Nina shook away the painful memory, surprised at how vivid and raw it still was. "I wasn't there for the plea. She asked me not to be and I respected her wishes. I went to the movies with a good friend of ours and tried not to think about what was happening across town. When I got back to our apartment, Franco had moved out and I never saw her again. It's one of the biggest regrets of my life."

"Wait." Lennox set down her glass and leaned forward with her elbows on the table. "You were in love with this woman, and she gets in trouble and walks out of your life and you didn't try to find her and make her change her mind? That doesn't sound like you."

"I was different then. You've never met my parents, but if you had you'd understand. I was raised to think money and status were the most important traits a person could have. At the time, I thought I was being a big rebel by getting a liberal arts degree and living with my girlfriend off campus instead of pledging Pi Phi and living on sorority row." She lowered her head. "I was a fraud. When it mattered, I caved and told myself letting Franco go was best for both of us because it's what she wanted."

"You may not want to hear this, but that might be true. It sounds like she had a problem. It wasn't your job to fix her if she wasn't interested in fixing herself."

"I don't think it's that simple." Nina slowly tore her napkin into long, jagged shreds while she contemplated exactly how complicated it was.

"You still care about her, don't you?"

"I don't know." The lie fell from her lips like a well-practiced line. "I don't even know her anymore." She fiddled with the pieces of dead napkin. "I can tell you that the Franco I saw today and last doesn't seem like the same person I remember. Of course, neither am I, so it doesn't really matter." Lennox pointed at the remaining fries on her plate, but Nina shook her head, her appetite gone. Lennox's question echoed in her mind against the backdrop of a now familiar scene that had been playing on a loop in her head. Franco, standing across the courtroom, staring into her eyes right before the shots rang out, and the ensuing parade of regrets that came when a person knew their life was in mortal danger. On the hit list of top regrets, Franco was still number one, and Nina was not at all sure what to do with that blockbuster bit of information.

CHAPTER NINE

Franco used a rubber mallet to pound the lid securely on the can of stain and tucked it into a corner of the deck. She'd managed to get a single coat applied while Pop was sleeping, but it was humid outside and she'd likely have to wait a day or more to apply the second layer.

When she walked back into the house, Pop was still dozing in the recliner. She tiptoed to her bedroom and changed into clothes that weren't coated in mahogany brown and signed on to her laptop to check her email. After firing off a few responses, she opened a new browser and typed Devon Grant's name into the search engine only to find no new developments since the last time she'd searched. She pulled up the website for Dallas County criminal records to see if anyone had entered an appearance on his behalf, but the space next to his name for defense lawyer was blank. She tapped her fingers on the desk and ran through a list of what she knew about his case.

Devon and his girlfriend, Lacy, daughter of Dallas oilman Harry Benton, both attended Richards University where they were freshmen. The evening Lacy had gone missing, she and Devon had been at a party thrown by his fraternity. Franco filed that fact away to ask Jenna more about the composition of the fraternity and how close Devon was to his Greek family.

And what about money? Jenna had made a big deal about how she didn't have a lot of money. How did Devon afford Greek life? She filed that question away as well.

Wait. There would be no filing away questions to be asked later. She'd promised to send Jenna a short list of good lawyers—lawyers who wouldn't be inextricably linked to both the mother of the defendant and the judge and have a poor relationship with the latter.

But would it hurt to have some perspective on the case first? How else would she know which other lawyer might be the perfect fit?

She knew her excuses were feeble ones, but her own strong curiosity won out and she reread several press accounts of the crime.

The last time anyone saw Lacy, she was arguing with Devon, which was of course why the police had focused on him as the primary suspect. It didn't help that when questioned the next morning, Devon had only a fuzzy recollection of anything that had happened the night before.

The real question was why were the police questioning anyone only hours after Lacy was last seen? Her roommate noticed she hadn't come home, but she was in college and old enough to be out as late as she wanted. Who had filed the missing person's report and how did they capture the attention of the police so quickly?

Franco went to the Dallas Police Department website and did a search on 911 calls only to find that unless requested by an individual or agency, the calls were only kept for thirty days. She opened the notes app on her phone and took a moment to write down all of the questions she had so far, including a note to remind her to ask the police department if anyone had submitted a request for the call records or filed a discovery motion with the prosecutor.

She scrolled through a few more articles about the case, settling on one that contained several interviews with Devon's fraternity brothers, most of which expressed outrage that Devon had been accused of murder coupled with outrage at him if he did what he was being accused of. She noted the names listed in the article and the irony of his so-called brothers failing to be there for him. Did Devon even like these guys or was he only in the fraternity to fulfill a legacy?

You could ask him.

She could've if a gunman hadn't shot up the courtroom.

You could go see him now.

She could, but what would be the point? She wasn't taking the case, and as soon as she got her dad back on track, she'd be heading home to Houston. She closed out her search and shut down her laptop, determined to quit thinking about Devon Grant and his plight, but the questions kept niggling at the edge of her consciousness no matter how much she tried to shift her focus away from them.

The jail was only a few miles away. With her bar card, she could go there and be back in a couple of hours tops.

Decision made, she grabbed her keys off the coffee table and stopped by the living room to spy Pop leaning all the way back and snoring his head off. She penned a quick note to say she'd be back soon and left it on the tray table beside him.

The jail was both different and the same as she remembered it. She'd only spent a few nights here, but it had been enough to leave an indelible impression on her, and as she got closer to the bank of doors leading into the horrible maze that was the Lew Sterrett Justice Center, her palms started sweating and her throat started to close.

"Excuse me, aren't you Franco Rossi?"

She turned toward the voice. Lennox, Nina's friend. The one who'd been surly toward her in the courtroom and at the hospital. Maybe she thought of Nina as more than a friend. No, wait, she'd had another woman with her at the hospital. Or maybe that person was the friend and Nina was something more. There was a lot she didn't know. "I am. And you're Lennox."

Lennox raised her eyebrows in approval and nodded. "You headed to the jail?"

Franco shifted her gaze to the line of people heading into the place she'd once been so anxious to leave. She'd been in many jails during her career, but she'd never been back to this one, and she hadn't given any thought to how it would affect her until right now when she was standing in front of it. She should turn and walk away, but with Lennox standing right there, she couldn't bring herself to duck the challenge. "Yes. You?"

"I'm meeting with a witness who happens to be in custody. Walk with me?"

"Sure." Franco accepted the invite, but she wasn't entirely sure it was altruistic. She kept up with Lennox's long strides as they walked through the meandering hallways that wove through the building, wary of both the destination and her companion on the journey.

"What brings you here?"

"To the jail?"

"To the jail, to Dallas, to Nina's courtroom."

Franco took note of how easily Lennox used Nina's first name and registered this wasn't a business-related question. "You two are close."

"She's my best friend."

"Then I can assume she's told you we have a past."

"Yes. Yes, you can."

"And you're here to warn me not to mess up her life."

"Something like that."

Franco observed the hard set of Lennox's jaw and decided the best course of action would be to set her mind at ease. "Then you'll be relieved to know I came to Dallas to meet with a client. I had no idea his case had landed in Nina's court until about five seconds before the shooting started." She stopped walking and turned to face Lennox square on. When she was certain she had her full attention, she said, "I wish nothing but the best for Nina. She deserves only good things."

Lennox held her gaze for a moment and then nodded. "Agreed. Do you think you're one of the good things?"

Franco laughed. Lennox's lack of subtlety was refreshing. "Does it matter what I think? I'm pretty sure you've already decided I'm not."

Lennox held up her hands. "Nina makes her own decisions about who she likes and who she doesn't. I only care about her not getting hurt."

"Then we're on the same page."

"Okay."

Lennox drew out the word, like it wasn't okay at all, but Franco wasn't in the mood to explain to this total stranger the reasons she'd made the decisions she had years ago. But she did have some questions of her own. "You know anything about the Lacy Benton case?"

Lennox's eyes flashed with intense interest. "Is that why you're in town?"

"Not entirely, but I'm looking into it."

"I haven't worked on it, if that's what you're asking, but I've heard the scuttle. The police arrested her boyfriend and from what I hear, they have the evidence to support an indictment. It's still pending with the grand jury, but I expect it'll be heard in the next week or so."

"Will one of your prosecutors be handling the case?" At Lennox's surprised look, she added, "Word is you were just promoted to super chief."

"Like 'just' as in last week. The day before the shooting. I haven't had a chance to meet with all of the ADAs on my watch to see what's pending yet."

Franco figured she was hedging and knew more, but there was no sense pushing the point if she wasn't sticking around to take the case. She pointed at the hallway to the right. "This is me. Thanks for the talk."

Lennox nodded. "Hope you're able to get back to Houston soon."

"Yeah, me too."

She didn't hear any footfalls behind her as she turned and walked down the hall and she wondered if Lennox was watching her go, but she couldn't worry about it. She'd meet with Devon, get a little more info, find him an attorney, and scratch this task off her list. One more step closer to returning to her life in Houston.

Five minutes later, she was sitting on a hard stool across from a plexiglass screen as Devon entered the room from the other side. She remembered being in the exact same position as him, sitting across from the public defender. Would Devon be like her, in full command of the facts and the possible consequences or would he be as muddled and confused as many of the defendants she'd represented over the years?

He picked up the handset and she did the same.

"Hey, Franco," he said.

The excitement in his voice was undeniable and she felt a pang of guilt that she was only here to gather information and not help him herself. "How are you holding up?"

"Well, I'm alive. Thanks to you. When do you think we can get a new bond hearing?"

She chose to ignore the "thanks to you" comment and take on the subject of the bond hearing head-on. "I imagine Judge Aguilar's docket is pretty backed up right now, and I've got to get back to Houston, but I thought it would be a good idea for you to tell me a bit more about the case—specifics I didn't want to hash out in the crowded holdover at the courthouse—and then I can find a good referral for you."

"Oh." The disappointment at her announcement she was moving on was palpable. He hung his head. "Hate to tell you this, but I don't know anything."

"You don't know anything, or you don't remember anything?"

"Like there's a difference," he said, his tone sullen.

"Trust me, there is." She pushed up from her chair. "You don't have to talk to me. If you'd rather wait until your mom hires someone else, that's cool." She waited a moment, but when he didn't respond, she turned and took the two steps between her chair and the door.

"Wait."

She didn't turn, but she stood perfectly still. Whatever happened next was in his hands.

"I don't remember what happened." He choked out a sob. "Hell, I don't even remember *if* anything happened. I was at the house for a mixer and of course Lacy was there. One minute we were making out in the corner and the next thing I remember was waking up in my room. Alone, and with a next-level hangover."

Franco narrowed her eyes. He was earnest, but was it an act to cover a heinous crime or was his sincerity born of a complete inability to remember the events? "Loss of memory is a regrettable inconvenience."

"Tell me about it. The cops don't believe me and I'm sensing you don't either."

"What I believe isn't important."

"Right."

"Seriously, Devon. I don't have any power here. I can't get your case dismissed, and if you believe an attorney works harder for you because they believe your story, that's nonsense. Attorneys will work hard for you because they're competitive, and trust me, you want that more than someone to believe in you."

"I don't even know you."

"True, but I have nothing to gain by showing up here."

"I guess. Besides my mom, you're the only person who's shown up to see me or even reached out."

"None of your fraternity brothers has been to see you?"

"No. It's like I've got the plague."

Franco considered his answer, unable to put her finger on why it bothered her. Something else bothered her too. "You said you woke up with a really bad hangover."

"Yeah, kind of. It was weird. No headache or puking, but I was super foggy and my mouth was desert dry."

"What did you have to drink at the party?"

"Beer, probably."

"Was there a keg?"

"Duh, fraternity house."

"Tell me everything you do remember."

He leaned back in his chair and relayed the basic facts, and they were really basic. He lived at the fraternity house, so he was there when they started setting up for the mixer. He had a beer while they were setting up, which probably meant he had a couple, but he insisted he'd only had one more after Lacy arrived before his memory blackout.

"Did you pull the beer yourself or was someone else working the keg?"

"I pulled my own before the party started, but then the

brothers assigned one of the other pledges to be tied to the keg for the night."

"Who was it?"

"The pledge on the keg?" He frowned. "Arnie Landeau. Nice guy, but kind of goofy."

"You remember that pretty well."

"Yeah, I guess so."

"Anything else you remember after that? Think really hard."

He stared at some point over her shoulder for a moment, not meeting her eyes. "Not really, no. It started getting hot in the room at some point. I think I may have told Lacy I was going outside to get some fresh air." He squinted like he was trying to conjure up a memory, and then shrugged. "That's it."

"What about Lacy's family? Any allies there?"

"Not even. Lacy's dad has always been nice to me in public, but his comments have an edge to them. Like I'm an okay for now boyfriend. You know, until Lacy finds someone better."

"I get it. Is it more protective father or asshole?"

He looked surprised at her choice of words. "Maybe a little of both."

She nodded while her mind started spinning with the theory that was already starting to form about what might have happened at the frat party. She pulled out her phone and opened a new note. "Give me a list of names, and if you remember phone numbers, even better. Anyone you can think of who was at the party."

He rattled off what he knew, and she wrote everything down. Dutifully, like she was his attorney. Which she wasn't. She'd hand these notes over to someone else. Someone she'd recommend to take his case. Someone she hoped would root out the truth because she had a feeling that no one investigating this case had bothered to look at all the angles, and it was going to take an aggressive lawyer to force law enforcement off their go-to position of the boyfriend did it. A quick mental scroll through her contact list didn't net any obvious results, but she was determined to get Devon the representation he needed because her gut told her this case was much more complicated than the police believed.

When she walked out of the jail, she stood in the courtyard between the jail and the courthouse and breathed in the cool, fresh air. If she turned to the right, she could walk straight to her car parked in the large lot on the south side of the building. It was the easiest, most direct route—the one her brain urged her to take. But her gut had her staring at the looming building in front of her. The one Nina was probably in. The one where she'd narrowly escaped being shot just last week, the one that had changed the direction of her future many years ago. Everything about this building was a threat to the careful life she'd managed to make for herself, but it also beckoned in a way that she could not deny.

Before she could analyze all angles of her decision, she started walking, and seconds later, she was pushing through the glass doors of the courthouse, toward whatever fate chose to offer next.

CHAPTER TEN

Nina looked up from her desk to see Reggie standing in the doorway of her temporary office. "Hey, Reggie."

"Hi, Judge." She hefted a stack of files with her good arm. "I pulled the docket for tomorrow. Do you want it now or should I put it on the bench?"

"Here's fine." Nina shoved a stack of papers to the side of her desk as Reggie walked toward her. "I'm probably going to be here for a while anyway."

"If it makes you feel any better, I've never seen anyone else run two dockets at the same time as efficiently as you. I've never seen anyone run one docket as efficiently as you run both of these. If the voters knew how efficient you are, Donaldson wouldn't have a chance."

The election. Right. Nina hadn't thought about the election in days, and even though the next two months would likely fly by, she wasn't ready to shift focus from her current chaos back to the chore of getting reelected. "I'm pretty sure any energy I have right now is fueled purely by adrenaline. Stick around because I might be running out of steam by the end of the week. Don't tell the voters." She added a smile, but what she really wanted to do was lay her head on her desk and sleep.

"No one expects you to do anything other than keep an eye on Larabee's cases. I put his on the top of the pile, sorted by age. There's only a couple where he'd be pushing for a disposition. The rest are straightforward and can be reset."

Nina nodded at her, but the declaration that no one expected much of her when it came to covering Larabee's docket rankled. "Knowing Judge Larabee, he'll be back at work before the doctor releases him, and I'd like to leave him with less work than he had when he left. Call it my small contribution to everyone's sanity."

"This is why everyone calls you Ms. Nice Judge." Reggie's hand flew to her mouth immediately following the statement and her wide eyes said she hadn't meant to share that particular tidbit out loud.

"Is that so?" Nina grinned. "Guess a lot of people get an unpleasant surprise when they find out I'm a lot tougher than they expected."

"Yes, ma'am."

"Don't call me that."

"Excuse me, what?"

"Don't call me ma'am." Nina infused the words with as much gravity as she could muster.

"Sorry, m—Sorry."

"I'm kidding. Well, mostly. I hate being called ma'am. Not sure why, but I do. As for the nice moniker, I don't mind. I'm as tough or tougher than any other judge in this building, but I don't see any reason to be a bully about it. If I choose to deliver harsh sentences politely and without acrimony and get called nice for it, I can live with that."

"Fair enough. No ma'aming you; nice doesn't equal soft. Got it."

Reggie delivered the words with a grin that Nina couldn't help but return. "Any word on the investigation?" she asked, certain Reggie would know exactly what investigation she was talking about.

"Rumors mostly, but the word is DPD is focused on Walt Ferguson and his pals."

Nina recognized the name, but it took her a moment to conjure up the relevance. "The open plea set in my court that morning?"

"That's the one. You know he was arrested with two other guys, but one of the perps was never arrested. The working theory is the unapprehended suspect is the shooter."

Nina cocked her head like it would help her process, but she couldn't wrap her head around the idea. "So, this guy Latamore is in the wind, but then he shows back up at a place where there are tons of law enforcement, so he can shoot up a courtroom and then run back into hiding. What was he supposed to accomplish?"

Reggie shrugged. "Good question. DPD thinks he either wanted to free Walt or shut him up. Maybe he figured Walt might try and score some points at his plea by telling the prosecutor where to find him, but when he showed up in the courtroom, Walt wasn't there—he was still in the holdover and if he'd tried to go in there, he would've risked getting trapped. All Marty or one of the other sheriff's deputies would've had to do was shut him in there until help arrived. The whole snafu with the elevator being out of service that morning and delaying Ferguson getting to the courtroom must have thrown Latamore off course."

Nina nodded. On the face of it, the theory made some sense, and it wasn't like criminals were always the smartest folks in the room, so the idea this Latamore guy would go to such great lengths to either free or kill a co-defendant wasn't that far-fetched. Still, something felt off. "Have they at least explored other angles?"

"Not entirely sure," Reggie said. "I do know that Harry Benton put up a sizeable reward for any information that leads to the apprehension of the shooter. DPD had to hire a temp to handle all the calls, but I hear most of them are attention-seeking crackpots."

"You sound like you have an inside track at the department," Nina said, impressed at Reggie's fact-finding.

Reggie pointed at her shoulder. "I have a vested interest." She paused. "Actually, I've always considered joining the force. I guess hanging out with cops is the next best thing."

"Don't go getting any ideas about leaving me to fight crime. At least not until Judge Larabee gets back." Nina smiled to show she was mostly kidding, and she was mid-smile when a linebacker-sized man in a sharply tailored suit appeared in the doorway of her office. "Can I help you?" she asked, figuring it was a defense attorney from out of town who'd lost his way.

"You're Judge Aguilar, aren't you?"

His voice was gruff and decidedly unfriendly. Nina watched Reggie square her shoulders and step directly in front of him. "Who are you?" Reggie asked.

"A taxpayer. Is that enough to get me in for a few words with the judge whose salary I pay?"

"Sir, I'd be happy to schedule an appointment with you to discuss any concerns you may have as long as you don't have a case pending in my court, but you'll need to go through the proper channels." Nina stood to give her words the force of her full presence and signal to this guy there would be no unscheduled sit-down with the judge today.

"When will Larabee be back?" the man asked, side-stepping Reggie, and walking farther into the room. "I'd like to talk to the real judge."

"I'm sure you would," Nina said, already over this

encounter. "But you'll have to do that another time. Now, I'm going to need you to leave or one of the sheriff's deputies will see you out."

"Is this how you treat all fathers of dead daughters? Or just the really rich ones who support the candidate running against you?"

Nina let his words play in a loop for a moment while she tried to place his face. It didn't take long. She'd never met Harry Benton in person, but his face graced the cover of local magazines and his photo routinely appeared in the social section of the news—her Sunday morning secret pleasure. He'd been in the news even more recently, following the murder of his only daughter, Lacy Benton. "Mr. Benton, I'm incredibly sorry for your loss, but you of all people should understand that after what happened in my courtroom last week, we're not going to tolerate unannounced visits to chambers. I get that you're grieving, and no one blames you for your state of mind, but it's improper for you to attempt to talk to me while your daughter's case is pending in my court."

"You bet I'm grieving." He shook a fist at her. "And you better do the right thing by my daughter. No bond for that scum of a boyfriend. He was never good enough for her and now he's taken her away from me forever."

His voice broke on the last words, and he stared at a spot on the wall like he'd lost his way. Nina wanted to comfort him, but it not only wasn't her job, her position specifically prevented her from doing anything other than offering up the few words she'd already delivered on the subject. She looked over at Reggie, who shook her head, held her hand to her head like she was talking on the phone and mouthed "sheriff"?

Nina gave Benton one last chance to leave on his own. "Mr. Benton, please don't make me call the sheriff."

He snapped his head back to her and the vacant look from a moment ago had been replaced by a fierce stare. "No need. I've said my piece. But know this. If my daughter's killer is not brought to justice, there will be hell to pay." He stormed out of the room before either she or Reggie could respond, and in the wake of his departure, Nina wasn't sure whether to laugh at the absurdity of a rich white man storming into her office to boss her around or be insulted at his implication she wasn't doing her job.

"What the hell was that?" Reggie asked, her hand immediately flying to her mouth. "Sorry, Judge."

"Don't be. I was about to say the same thing. I mean really. Did he ever storm in on Larabee like that?"

Reggie shook her head. "He wouldn't dare. Don't know if you know much about the guy, but he's known for being uber conservative, and part of that is thinking women should be obedient. While he wouldn't try that stunt on Judge Larabee, he sure thought his shock and awe would work on you. Way to stand up to him."

"It's not like he's going to vote for me no matter what I do," Nina said, smiling to defuse the tension Benton had left behind. She waved at the stack of work on her desk. "I'm going to stick around and see if I can get caught up, but you should call it a day."

Reggie pointed at her and back at her own chest. "You stay, I stay. I've got plenty to do and could use the extra time at my desk. Let me know when you're done, and we can walk out together. You know, in case Mr. Rich Guy decides to come back. I'll be at my desk if you need me."

After Reggie left her office, Nina had a hard time concentrating, but she was determined to push through. She focused all her energy on the files in front of her, determined to get a handle on tomorrow's lineup, and she'd finally managed to get into a rhythm when raised voices outside her office distracted her.

"Her office is right there, correct?"

"That's none of your business. If you want to see the judge, you can schedule an appointment."

"Tell her Franco Rossi is here to see her."

"You can come back tomorrow."

"I strongly suggest you tell her I'm here."

"And I strongly suggest you back off. Maybe you didn't hear, but there was a shooting here last week and we don't take kindly to people trying to push their way into places they don't belong."

Nina was up and out of her chair when she heard Franco's voice, and now that she heard the exchange escalating, she rushed toward the door and flung it open. Reggie was standing guard with her arms crossed and Franco was right up in her personal space like she was itching for a fight.

"Franco, get in here right now."

Reggie shot her a confused look and she scrambled for a plausible excuse for intervening. "My fault. I scheduled this appointment myself. Next time, I'll make sure any appointments go through you. Sorry."

She grabbed Franco by the arm and ushered her into her chambers, closing the door behind them. She waited until she heard Reggie's footfalls fade away before launching in.

"What are you doing here?"

"Nice to see you too."

"In case you hadn't noticed, there was a shooting here last week and we're all a little on edge, so barging your way into my office probably wasn't the best plan to win friends and influence people."

Franco squinted her eyes. "Damn. I'm sorry. I should've known better."

Nina held back an "it's okay" and traded it for a question. "Is there some reason you keep showing up in my space? First the hearing last week, then the grocery store, now here? If you have something on your mind, please get it off your chest and go back to your other life. You know, the one you created completely without me."

Franco's jaw dropped. "You make it sound like I was off partying. I was in jail and then on probation."

"And then you weren't." She trembled with anger and took a breath to still the quake. "While I was wondering why you stopped taking my calls, you apparently reenrolled in school, graduated, and went on to get a law degree. Of course, these are mere suppositions on my part because I have no personal knowledge about anything to do with your life and I haven't for a very long time. Which begs the question again—why do you keep showing up in mine?"

Nina took a breath. She hadn't meant to say any of these things out loud, and she wasn't sure she'd realized how close her anger was to the surface until Franco strode back into her life like nothing had gone wrong between them. There was a time Franco had been a calming and comforting influence, but that had changed after she'd turned both of their worlds upside down.

"I'm sorry."

Franco's tone was dejected, but the eyes staring at her were earnest and sincere. Against her better judgment, Nina believed her. Too bad it was too late. "Okay." It was all she could muster.

"Can we talk?" Franco asked. "About something other than us?"

Please. "You have a particular topic in mind?"

"I do."

Nina gestured to the chairs across from her desk and they settled across from each other. Franco leaned forward with her hands on her knees.

"What's so important you came all the way down here to talk to me about?"

"Harry Benton's daughter, Lacy."

Nina stiffened. "What about her?"

"I've been looking into the case."

"Then you know I can't talk to you about it."

"Because it's assigned to you or because it's me asking?"

"Definitely because it's assigned to me, even if it's only until Judge Larabee is back. As for not being able to talk to you specifically, I guess that depends on why you're asking. Is this the case you were in court for last week? I heard the defendant was still trying to raise funds to hire an attorney. Surely, he can't afford your fees."

Franco cocked her head. "You don't know, do you?"

Nina was annoyed at the vague question. "Know what?"

"The defendant is Devon Grant."

Nina's agitation ramped up at Franco's insistence on being vague. "And?"

"He's Jenna's son."

She opened her mouth to say she still didn't know what Franco was talking about, but then everything stalled into a slow-motion reel and all she could do was watch it play out. "Jenna's son. Devon."

"Yes."

"Devon is the defendant. Charged with murdering his girlfriend, Harry Benton's daughter." Nina heard herself speak the words out loud, but she was having trouble digesting the information and Franco was staring at her like she'd grown a second head.

"Are you okay?"

Nina stood and started pacing. "I haven't seen you in years, and Jenna and I haven't spoken in almost as long, yet within a week, my courtroom gets shot to pieces and then I get this blast from the past right on top of it. No, I'm not okay."

Franco reached for her hand. "Sit down, let's talk."

Nina looked down at her hand in Franco's. Familiar, warm, safe. Their hands, clasped together, felt everything but right and she forced herself to pull back, folding her hands in her lap before they could betray her again. She sank into the chair across from Franco. Sitting was good and simple and no one got in trouble from simply sitting. She slid back into the seat. "I'm listening."

Franco crossed and uncrossed her legs, a stall tactic for sure. When she finally settled in and leaned back in her chair, her first question took Nina by surprise. "Why haven't you seen Jenna?"

It was a legit question. She, Jenna, and Franco had been fast friends in college, and when Franco suddenly dropped out, Jenna was the one she leaned on for support. But that had been years ago, and she hadn't talked to Jenna since... Anyway, she certainly didn't know Jenna had a son, but she wasn't sure why she should care. After her last encounter with Jenna, she didn't much care about anything that might be going on in her life. "How old is Devon?"

"He's nineteen."

The number rang a bell and Nina did the math. The last time she'd spoken to Jenna had been freshman year in college. She remembered the crisp, cool winter air. They'd been standing in the courtyard of their dorm. Franco had left over the winter break and the spring semester had just begun. She'd been unable to concentrate on her studies, and Jenna's solution was to coax her out of her room with the promise that fresh air would heal all wounds.

"Come on," Jenna said. *"Let's go for a walk."*

"I need to focus." Nina kept her head down, staring at the calculus text full of equations she'd likely never put to any use. She'd been "studying" for hours but couldn't conjure up one thing she'd learned other than a broken heart impeded all ability to focus. It had been two weeks since she'd last seen Franco, but it felt like years. When would the pain stop?

"How's that going for you?"

Nina looked up to see Jenna's grin and she couldn't help but grin back. "Pretty lousy, but I figure if I work at it, I'll get better."

Jenna titled the blind open and pointed at the window. "It's a beautiful day. The sun is shining, and you can smell winter in the air." She reached over and plucked the textbook from Nina's hands. "I insist."

Nina sighed. Maybe a walk and some fresh air would do her good. "Fine, but I have to be back in an hour. I've been staring at that book all day and I still don't know how to solve a single problem."

Jenna crossed her heart. "I promise to have you back to your boring text in short order."

Nina pulled on her coat and boots and followed Jenna downstairs. The courtyard was empty, and the only sound was the light rustling of the last leaves of fall. It was the kind of day Franco would've made special with an impromptu picnic, and she closed her eyes for a moment and imagined what it would be like to roll back time to the beginning of the fall semester when they'd both been full of hope and promise and certain their futures would always be intertwined.

"It's beautiful, right?"

Jenna's voice penetrated her thoughts and reminded her that she wasn't here with Franco. Franco had left her, and she wasn't sure if she'd ever even known her at all. She wasn't ready to see beauty in the void, but it was impolite not to acknowledge Jenna's efforts to make her feel better. "It's nice."

"Come on then."

Jenna reached for her hand, and she didn't resist. They walked, hand in hand, away from the dorm toward the quad. When they reached the fountain in the middle, Jenna motioned to a bench and suggested they have a seat. After they settled in, Jenna fidgeted in her seat and cleared her throat.

"I have something I want to tell you."

Nina stiffened at the announcement. "No good ever came after a pronouncement like that."

"It's nothing bad. I promise." Jenna ducked her head. "In fact, I'm hoping you think it's as exciting as I do."

"Let me guess. You finally decided which of the guys at the Sig Ep house you're going to marry."

"Hardly."

Jenna glanced away and kicked her toe at an imaginary pebble on the ground. Nina noted the pink in her cheeks intensify. Was she nervous or only cold? "Are you going to make me pull it out of you?"

"Maybe." Jenna shrugged. "I don't know why this is so hard. I spent all day thinking about what I wanted to say and how I was going to say it. Now that the time has come, I'm crazy nervous."

Nina's nerves kicked in. Something about Jenna's demeanor had her completely on edge. She braced for whatever. "Okay, spill."

Jenna cleared her throat and squared her shoulders. *"I know it's only been a few weeks since Franco left, and I know how sad you've been."*

"Okay."

"You don't have to look at me like I'm about to stab you." Jenna gave her a lopsided grin. *"Far from it."*

Nina resisted the urge to roll her hand to urge Jenna to get to the point. Whatever this point was, she sensed it was going to be painful and she wasn't sure she wanted to hear it at all.

"Please tell me what's going on."

"I love you." Jenna's grin morphed into a big, bright smile. *"I've always loved you. I never said anything because you were infatuated with Franco, but she was never right for you and you know that now."* She reached out and grabbed Nina's hand. *"We could have a wonderful future. You as a lawyer and me as a doctor. We'll be a power couple. And I know you might need more time to get past what you had with Franco, but I think you'll see that what happened was ultimately the best thing that could happen. Our futures will be bright. Together."*

A cold chill settled over Nina at the first I love you, and she was a block of ice by the end. She needed to say something. Anything to dispel the fantasy Jenna had built up about them, but all she could do was sit, paralyzed, wondering what she'd done to contribute to the notion their relationship was anything more than friendship. She racked her brain but couldn't come up with anything other than Jenna had lost her mind.

She stood abruptly, pulling her hand back from Jenna's like she was dodging a viper. *"I have to go."*

"Wait," Jenna called out. *"Aren't you going to say anything?"*

Franco's voice played in her head, teasing her that Jenna

had always had a crush on her, to which she'd always replied that Jenna was super straight and straight girls were weird that way. She had never, not once, taken the teasing seriously, but right now her mind whirred through an examination of every conversation, every interaction she'd ever had with Jenna in a quest to determine what she'd missed. Had she really been that naive?

"I don't even know where to begin." Nina stared at Jenna who clearly wasn't getting the rebuff, so she pressed harder. "There is no us and there never will be. We're friends. At least I thought we were."

Jenna stood and walked toward her. "We could be so much more if you would simply open your mind to the idea. I know you need time and I'm willing to wait, but I wanted you to know I'm here, ready for what comes next."

Nina took a step to the side, hoping she wouldn't have to sprint away to make her point. "Not going to happen. For God's sake, Jenna. Franco was the love of my life. Have you really thought all this time that she's no good for me? That I would be better off with you? What kind of a friend are you?"

"The kind who sits around and waits for you to come to your senses. Tell me I didn't waste my time."

"You absolutely did." Nina shook her head. "I'm leaving now. Don't follow me. I need space and I need to be alone." She walked briskly away, ignoring Jenna's pleas.

Nina shook her head. "I can't believe she has a son. He had to have been born the year you and I broke up. Hell, she barely waited a month after you left before professing her undying love for me."

"Excuse me?"

Franco looked genuinely surprised. "I guess all those

times you teased about how she had a crush on me were spot-on," Nina said.

"Oh, wow. I really was teasing. Although, if she really did profess her true love for you, I can see now that all of those overtures were the real deal."

"I had no idea. None. A few weeks after the spring semester started, she decided she had to come clean."

"That explains a lot," Franco said, nodding.

"How so?"

"She encouraged me to break up with you. Told me it was the best thing for both of us. That I'd only hold you back."

"And you listened to her?"

"Damn it, Nina, I was nineteen years old. Your parents were all over you to break up with me. You were doing everything in your power to convince me not to go to the cops."

"If you'd only listened."

"I didn't have a choice."

Nina stared into Franco's deep, dark eyes, willing her to explain why she would surrender her own future and theirs as a couple. Why hadn't their love been worth fighting for?

But she couldn't go there. Not now, not after so much time and distance had come between them. Besides, she didn't know anything about Franco. Not anymore. "So, you went to law school."

Franco cracked a smile. "You could say I was inspired by current events at the time. I got my probation transferred to Harris County and enrolled at the University of Houston— they had a special program for 'at-risk' students. I worked my ass off doing food delivery while I was in undergrad, and the money from that and a big stack of student loans got me through Rice law school."

"You live in Houston?"

"I have an apartment and office there, but I've taken cases around the state." She looked around. "This is the first time I've been back to this courthouse, though." She held up her hands. "Don't get the impression I'm stalking you. I took Jenna's call for old times' sake. I had no idea you were a judge here and not a clue this case would wind up in your courtroom."

"Are you taking it?"

"Devon's case?" Franco hesitated and glanced away. "I told Jenna no."

Nina heard the slight equivocation. Franco telling Jenna no wasn't the same as telling her right here and now. "But you're thinking about it."

"It is intriguing."

What's intriguing is why you showed up in my life again. "Wait, did you think you could press me for details about the case? Is that why you stopped by?"

"I'd be lying if I said that hadn't factored in. I'm not looking for specific details, but it wouldn't hurt to know your impression of the prosecutor, the investigation."

Franco's request wasn't entirely unreasonable. Nina had had casual conversations with Lennox about cases—it was kind of the norm among the regulars who worked at the courthouse. But Franco wasn't a regular and she wasn't sure she wanted her here at all. Any conversation they had would be fraught with the peril of the personal rift between them, and she wasn't interested in going there. Not anymore. "I think you better go. If you're even thinking about taking this case, we can't be in chambers like this."

A quick frown crossed Franco's face, but it was quickly covered by her trademark grin. She stood. "Fair enough, but I'm taking that to mean that if I don't take this case, then we *can* be in chambers like this." She strode to the door without waiting on a response, and delivered one last line before exiting. "I'll be in touch."

The door had barely closed before Nina put her head in her hands. "What the actual hell was that?" Franco Rossi had walked out of her life once again, but this time she should've known better than to let her in in the first place.

CHAPTER ELEVEN

Franco stood at the door of the exam room and peered inside where Pop was fiddling with the strings of his paper gown. She was torn between thinking she should take over or letting him retain some semblance of independence, but even getting him to come to the doctor at all had been a challenge.

"Don't you have a friend that's a doctor? Maybe she'll make a house call."

"No, Pop. No doctor friends here in Dallas."

He shook his head and his brow wrinkled into a frown like he was digging deep for a memory. "I swear you did. Jenna— that's her name. Give her a call. I don't want to go see some stranger."

It had been frustrating enough dealing with his lack of short-term recall, but to have him muster up an almost twenty-year-old memory of Jenna saying she wanted to go to med school someday was next-level annoying. She'd replayed yesterday's conversation with Nina over and over, growing angrier each time at Jenna's power play in both convincing her breaking up with Nina was the kindest thing she could do, and then barely waiting until she was out of Nina's life before making her move. The nerve of Jenna to call years later, asking for help for her son. Did Jenna really think she'd never find out about her betrayal?

Apparently so. Of course, Jenna's life appeared to have taken a sharp turn around the same time hers had. Based on Devon's age, Jenna had given birth to him when she was a sophomore in college, and a quick background search didn't show any evidence she'd ever become a doctor like she'd planned.

Whatever. She didn't have the bandwidth to care about Jenna's life, especially not after she'd heard what Nina had to say. If anything, the revelation only made it easier to be free of the obligation to grant her any favors, and as soon as she got her dad's health issues squared away, she could get back to her life in Houston.

But Devon still needs help, and he didn't do anything to you.

She pushed the thought away. The only problem here in Dallas that was her responsibility to solve was the man on the other side of this door. She pushed her way into the room and sent a silent thanks to the heavens that Pop was still wearing pants. She gently pulled the gown around his concave chest and tied the strings.

"Thanks, Frances. I didn't know you were coming to visit."

She forced herself not to react to the lapse in memory but made a note of how these were occurring more often. Or maybe this was the new normal and she simply hadn't noticed because she hadn't been to visit in a while. The time between visits had become longer and longer over the years. She'd told herself she wasn't able to make the trip as often because she was busy with work, but she always made time to travel wherever she had to for work. The truth was it was painful to see him, even more so now because the long interval since the last visit only made all the signs of her neglect more obvious. She either needed to come to Dallas more often or hire someone to look after him. Feeling a bit like a coward, she made a note to ask Julie to put out feelers for a reputable agency.

The door opened as she finished typing the reminder into her phone, and when she turned, she was surprised to see a young woman standing in front of her wearing a white lab coat. The woman stuck out her hand.

"I'm Dr. Mason."

Franco stared at the hand for a moment before remembering her manners and grasping it with her own while she mentally calculated the lowest number of years old someone could be before becoming a physician. "Franco Rossi."

Dr. Mason smiled and motioned to her father. "And this is Mr. Rossi, I presume."

"Yes, he's my father. Dominic."

"Hello, Mr. Rossi."

"You're a young one," he announced, causing Franco to wince.

"He's not always like this," she said, promptly realizing it was a lie since she had no idea what he was really like these days. She was also a little embarrassed that he'd spoken out loud exactly what she'd been thinking.

The cute doctor laughed. "It's okay. I often get asked to send in the real doctor." She pointed at the chart in her hand. "I was reading over his symptoms before I came in. Does he schedule his own medications, or do you assist with that?"

Franco cleared her throat, but there was no avoiding her confession: she hadn't taken an interest in his care for a long time, ironic as it was. "He's been handling it. I live in Houston." She winced again at the lame excuse.

"That makes sense." Dr. Mason scribbled some notes on

the chart. "The things you've described—lapses in memory, chronic fatigue—may be caused by his meds being off. It could be a matter of him not taking them as prescribed or we might need to adjust his dosage. I'll order some blood work, but I'm willing to bet if we get his meds sorted out, he'll be back to normal in no time."

Franco matched the young doctor's smile, but all she could think was how she didn't really have a benchmark for normal when it came to her dad. She had a lot to learn.

They'd checked out with the receptionist and were walking to the car when Pop announced in a thundering voice that he was starving.

"I could eat," Franco said. "You have a place in mind?"

"There's a diner. Down by the trade center." He made a swirling motion above his head. "Waitresses are a throwback to the fifties."

"Market Diner." Franco laughed. The beehive hairdos worn by some of the staff weren't 1950s cosplay, but authentic style. "I love that place. And don't they serve breakfast all day?"

At his nod, she jangled her keys. The drive from Dr. Mason's office to the diner only took fifteen minutes, and since they'd beaten the lunch crowd, they didn't have to wait for a table, and within a few minutes after arriving, they'd ordered coffee and enough breakfast staples to send them both into a righteous food coma. While they waited for their food, Franco cast about for innocuous topics of conversation.

"It's supposed to rain this weekend. We should probably get a service out to clean the gutters."

"I can do it."

She nodded to pretend like she was considering the offer. Sending a stranger out to help him was going to be an issue since it was unlikely he'd remember why the contractor was showing up and would likely send him away. Hell, she'd already planned to stay for a bit—she may as well get some exercise while she was here. "How about we do it together?"

"Okay, Frances, but you'll have to do what I say because climbing on the roof can be dangerous."

She sighed at his instant relapse into parenting a teenager mode but resisted rolling her eyes. "Fine, Pop. Whatever you say."

"Maybe when you're done, you could invite your girlfriend over for dinner. I can make my famous chili. She loves it even if you think it's too spicy."

So, now he was remembering Nina. What fresh hell was this where her dad reverted to memories of people she was determined to forget? "She's not my girlfriend anymore, Pop. We don't even speak," she added, thinking it was easier to cut this off right now.

"Then why is she joining us for lunch?" He pointed over her shoulder, and she turned before she could contemplate the consequences. There was Nina, standing at the door to the restaurant, looking around. Three, two, one. Their eyes locked and, despite her resistance, Nina's intense stare captured her full attention.

"Nina, come join us."

Franco whipped her head back to see her dad grinning like crazy. "Pop," she hissed, but it was too late. The diner wasn't very big, and within a few seconds, Nina was standing next to their table looking like she'd just left a photoshoot for best-dressed businesswomen of Dallas in her perfectly tailored midnight blue suit.

"Hi, Pop," she said, reaching to take both of his hands in her own. "It's great to see you." Still holding his hands, she turned slightly and nodded. "Franco."

"Nina." She wanted to say more. Something along the

lines of great to see you or great suit—what a shame you have to cover it up with a judge's robe, but she decided to follow Nina's lead and wait to see if she was ready to break down the barriers between them.

"Sit, girl." Pop patted the seat beside him, and Franco silently echoed his invitation.

Nina's smile carried all the affection she'd always shown toward her parents, and Franco was instantly transported back to all the times Nina had joined her family around the kitchen table for dinner. Before Mom got sick and Pop lost his way.

"I'd love to join you, but I'm meeting a colleague for lunch. Maybe I can come by and visit you sometime after Frances goes back home."

After Frances goes back home. Ouch. Not only had Nina used the name she knew irritated her, but the reference to returning home was designed to send a message. A message Franco chose to ignore. She started to say something about how she didn't bite, but Pop responded first.

"Frances?" His face was twisted with confusion. "But she's already home."

Uh-oh. Franco looked up, willing Nina to play along with his account of her current situation. "That's right. I'm sticking around for a while. Pop and I have a bunch of projects to get done around the house."

"Sounds great," Nina said with a clear lack of enthusiasm. She squeezed Pop's hands. "It was great to see you. I hope you and Franco have a nice time together."

She backed away from the table and turned to go. Franco watched her take a couple of steps, torn between letting her get back to her regularly scheduled life and wanting to disrupt it. "I'm sure we'll see each other again soon," she called out.

Pop joined the chorus. "Come for dinner. Friday night. I'll

make chili. You love my chili. Six p.m. on the dot. Don't bring anything. I've got it covered."

Nina's only answer was a tender smile directed entirely at Pop, and then a quick grimace in Franco's direction. Franco didn't blame her for being annoyed. She'd practically ghosted Nina before that was even a thing, and expecting her to forgive her instantly and lapse back into the life they'd led nineteen years ago wasn't realistic and it wasn't likely.

But fate had conspired to bring them together for some reason. Jenna's out-of-the-blue phone call asking for help for her son and Devon's case getting reassigned to Nina's court the day she showed up to meet him were obvious signs, but it went even deeper than that. If Franco had known about Jenna's betrayal of her years ago, would she have agreed to come to Dallas and meet her son? She might have gone her entire life never crossing paths with Nina again. Lord knows she'd tried hard not to. She'd made a successful life for herself, professionally, anyway, and she'd convinced herself she had everything she could need or want. But coming home meant facing reality. She might have built an ostensibly wonderful life for herself, but she'd neglected her dad and she'd let the woman she'd never stopped loving believe she was a fuck-up all these years. Sticking around might give her a chance to make things right with both of them, and even if Nina never forgave her, she'd be a better person for trying to make amends.

An image of Devon, sitting in the holdover, wearing a way-too-big jumpsuit and looking scared shitless, flashed in her mind. She could relate to the fear and she hated the idea he didn't have a worthy adversary on his side.

She could stick around. Get things started on his case, and then get someone local to handle court appearances until it was ready to go to trial, assuming that was the only resolution.

It wasn't Devon's fault his mother wasn't a good person. He was just a kid, and Franco had a soft spot for kids.

Because you were like him once.

Not really. I made a choice to be in the system. He didn't.

Unless he's guilty—that's a choice.

She shook her head. If Devon was guilty, the system would balance toward justice, but he'd need a good attorney to make sure the prosecution didn't have its thumb on the scale. If the local lawyers were scared off by Harry Benton's big purse strings, maybe an out-of-town lawyer was the perfect solution.

She looked around and spotted Nina sitting on a stool at the counter. She was alone and Franco made a split-second decision. "Be right back, Pop."

She was out of her seat before he could answer, determined to do this thing before she changed her mind. She strode up to Nina and sat on the stool next to hers. "Hi again."

"Yes, Frances?" Nina punctuated the question with a grin that either said she wasn't really mad at her or she was taking devilish glory in making her squirm.

"Fine. I'll let you call me Frances even though you know I hate it."

"'Let me'?"

Franco rolled her eyes.

"Seriously, Frances. Your given name is one of the only things I know about you anymore."

"We can change that."

Nina sighed. "No, we can't. I've moved on. It's been a very long time. You should move on too."

"I'm taking the case."

"What?"

Franco could swear she saw a glimmer of excitement on Nina's face, but it quickly morphed into the carefully formed neutral expression she'd been wearing since she arrived and spotted her at the restaurant. "Devon's case. I'm taking it. I'll file a formal appearance, but I wanted you to be the first one to know."

Nina's eyes widened and her mouth opened and closed in a wordless display of shock and confusion. Franco slid off the stool and backed away, still facing her. "Like I said, I'm sure we'll be seeing each other again soon."

As she walked back to her booth, the impact of her snap decision landed as her brain started whirring with all of the things she'd need to do to make this happen. *What's the big deal?* Last week, she'd been totally open to the idea of taking on an out-of-town case, and this wasn't the first or even the fifteenth long distance trial she'd handled.

But none of the others had a judge who happened to be her ex-girlfriend. This was going to get interesting fast.

"Frances?"

"What's up, Pop?"

"We need to go to the store. I need to get the stuff to make chili."

CHAPTER TWELVE

Nina shrugged out of her robe and replaced it with her new favorite piece of clothing, a midnight blue, metallic tweed blazer she'd snagged on sale at Neiman's. Larabee kept his office deep freezer cold, and her attempts to pry open the cover on the thermostat had only resulted in a broken nail file. Reggie had put in a work order, which meant the county might send someone to regulate the temperature by the following year if she was lucky. Thankfully, Larabee should be back way before then.

As if on cue, Reggie appeared in her doorway. "Come on in," Nina said, pointing at the files in Reggie's hand. "Please tell me those aren't more cases on the docket this afternoon. I desperately need to catch up on my paperwork and I've got a half dozen motions to review."

"Your docket is clear." Reggie handed her the files. "Both of those were delivered just now. One is a summary of the DPD investigation of the shooting so far, and the other one came from Tarrant County and it's in a sealed envelope. I wasn't sure if you wanted me opening your mail, so I didn't check it out."

"Whatever you do for Judge Larabee is fine with me."

After Reggie left, Nina peered at the second, mystery envelope for a moment before her memory kicked in. She'd requested the prosecutor's file on Lennox's brother's case from the archives in Tarrant County. Lennox and Wren had been looking into appealing his sentence, so she hadn't been convinced the prosecutor would turn over his file, but apparently, being a judge in a neighboring county had more perks than she'd anticipated. She set it aside and pulled the other file toward her.

It was thin. Not a good sign. She opened it and began skimming the three-page report. The masked shooter had been spotted by several eyewitnesses leaving her courtroom, but then he vanished. Based on the witness descriptions, he matched the general height and build of Walt Ferguson's cohort Latamore, but without anyone being able to see his face, there was no way to confirm his ID. The police recovered the guns, in pieces, at various spots in the courthouse, like a trail of criminal breadcrumbs, but the trail ran cold after all the gun parts were recovered. She turned to the last page, which didn't contain any more detail than the other two and ended with the words "investigation ongoing."

It didn't sound ongoing to her. It sounded like DPD had decided on a suspect and they were all in on finding Latamore. She suspected it was only a matter of time before they released their theory to the press with a mandate to the citizens of Dallas to find Latamore and turn him in.

The mention of press coverage spurred her to pull up Google and start a search. *Suspects in courthouse shooting. Dallas.* She sat back and watched while rows of results filled the screen. Mostly reports from the day of the shooting and human interest interviews after the fact, but nothing jumped out at her that might assist the investigation.

She started to turn back to the file, but her fingers paused over the keyboard, and the Google logo for the day dared her to put action to her thoughts. She heaved a heavy sigh and typed

"Dominic Rossi" into the search bar. Several records appeared, enough to confirm he still lived in Franco's childhood home. *Wonder if his chili is as good as I remember it?* Uh-oh. Pop's mention of chili and the dinner invitation were just the latest of several triggers, reminding her of what she'd once had with Franco and how devastating it had been when Franco walked away.

Don't get sucked in. Even if she takes Jenna's son's case, it will eventually be over and Franco will go back to Houston, to the life she chose not to share with you.

But it had been Pop who'd asked her to dinner, not Franco. He looked like he could use some socializing, and he had appeared to be very excited at the prospect of company for dinner, which reminded her she'd always had an open invitation to eat at the Rossis' when she and Franco were in high school. Even after Franco's mom was diagnosed with cancer, Franco's parents were always warm and welcoming, unlike her parents, who were stiff and judgmental. The idea of spending an evening revisiting some of the pleasant memories of her past was especially inviting, and who was she to deny Pop's adamant request?

When she finally finished enough paperwork to feel like she wasn't completely drowning, she drove home and changed into jeans and a dark blue sweater, one that wasn't likely to show chili if she wound up making a mess. She completed the look with a pair of mid-heel black suede booties, her favorite black leather jacket, and a pop of raspberry lipstick.

Franco's childhood home was in an older section of northeast Dallas, only a few miles from where she lived, but in the opposite direction from her usual haunts. The houses were 1950s bungalow-style homes, and the neighborhood was a mishmash of newly renovated properties and houses in disrepair. Pop's house was one of the latter and, after pulling into the driveway, she sat in her car for a moment and remembered the house the way it used to be—bright and well-kept.

A knock on the window jarred her out of her trip down memory lane, and she looked to her left to see Franco standing beside her car with a questioning look in her eyes. Her stomach sank at the notion she might have been the only one who'd thought Pop's invitation was legit, but she grabbed the bottle of wine she'd brought and climbed out of the car, anyway. "I'm guessing by the look on your face, there may not be a chili dinner waiting inside."

"Oh, there's a chili dinner all right, and Pop even remembers he invited you, which is more than he's remembered since I got here. I've spent the entire day trying to manage his expectations." Franco pointed at the bottle of wine in her hand. "Although I specifically recall he told you not to bring anything."

Nina shoved the bottle toward Franco. "I was running late, or I would've stopped for beer, but it's a hearty zin with enough heft to pair nicely with chili. If you don't want to open it, consider it a hostess gift." She shifted from one foot to the other, feeling a bit awkward now that she was here. "I guess I should've called to say I was coming, but the truth is I didn't think I was until about an hour ago."

Franco cocked her head. "Any chance you want to tell me what changed your mind?"

Nina smiled. "I really like Pop's chili."

Franco returned the smile. "That's a win for both of us." She waved her arm toward the front porch. "After you."

Nina walked up the stairs. The house might not look the same as it did when they were in high school, but the comfortable feeling of coming home felt exactly the same.

"I'm glad you changed your mind," Franco said as she walked up behind her and opened the door.

"I noticed you haven't filed an appearance in Devon Grant's case."

Franco abruptly shut the door before they could walk through. "Then I should let you know if that's the only reason you decided to show up for dinner, you might want to leave now before Pop sees you because a courier delivered the notice to the clerk's office late this afternoon. It's probably not even in the court file yet."

Nina stood in place, stymied by Franco's announcement. She'd let herself be lulled into thinking she could have a nice, pleasant evening revisiting her past, but if Franco really was taking Devon's case, she needed to guard against more than her own mixed feelings about the circumstances that had led her and Franco to break up all those years ago. Now, she had the present potential of the appearance of impropriety to worry about.

But there was no actual impropriety. It had been almost twenty years since she and Franco were involved, and she had less of a relationship with her now than she did with Lennox. Yet she wouldn't hesitate to have dinner with Lennox and think nothing about how it appeared.

This is different and you know it.

A second later, the front door flew open, surprising them both. Pop's grin was wide, and he was waving a very large, chili-soaked spoon in the air. "Nina! Come in. Dinner's almost ready." He held open the door and motioned for them to come inside. "We'll eat on the deck out back. You should see how nice it looks. Frances has been sanding and staining all week."

Nina shot a look at Franco, who shrugged.

"Hence the delay in getting court papers filed. It's been a

while since I did any DIY home repairs, but I think it turned out nice."

Nina looked from her to Pop and back again. If she was going to leave, now was the time, but the sharp smell of cumin, the bright smile on Pop's face, and the prospect of finally putting a piece of her past behind her were more enticing than she could resist. She turned to Franco. "I'll be the judge of that. Are you going to show me in or what?"

❖

Franco followed Nina and Pop into the house, wishing she'd spent more time tidying the inside instead of working on the deck this week. But the physical labor had been a welcome respite from hours of paperwork, both on her pending cases and dealing with organizing Pop's household bills and sorting out his medical benefits. The time she'd lost on those tasks was her own fault, a byproduct of not paying closer attention to his day-to-day, but she truly hadn't realized he'd stopped being able to handle the basics on his own. Hopefully, his situation would improve once they got him back on a routine, including the right dosage of meds, but for now she added finding a housekeeper to the growing list of taking care of Pop items.

When they reached the kitchen, Franco held up the bottle of wine Nina had brought. "You want a glass?"

Nina pointed at the refrigerator. "Only if there's no cold beer in there."

"As if." Franco reached in and pulled out two bottles, twisted off the caps, and handed one to Nina. She'd always loved that despite her posh upbringing, Nina didn't feel like she had to gussy up her drink choice, especially if it didn't fit the food or atmosphere. As for herself, she could appreciate a robust red wine with chili, but Pop's place was more six-pack than cork in a bottle.

Nina tilted her bottle toward Franco's and after the clink of glass, they each took a deep drink. Their eyes locked and for a moment, she searched for words to tell Nina how grateful, how happy she was to see her again, but before she could speak, Pop's voice broke the spell.

"Hey, you two, I hope you're hungry," he called out from across the room where he was adding the final touches to his pot of chili. "It's almost ready. I'm going outside to set up the deck. Frances, grab three of the extra-large soup bowls and get the fixins out of the fridge."

With mixed feelings about the interrupted moment, Franco reached into the cabinet and pulled down the bowls, pointing at the refrigerator with her free hand. "You heard the man. Get cracking."

Nina took one more swig of her beer and started pulling out the "extras." When she was done, containers of sour cream, shredded sharp cheddar cheese, chopped onion, and jalapeños lined the counter. Franco watched as she walked over to the pantry and scanned the shelves, and ultimately shut the door, empty-handed.

"What's wrong?" Franco asked, noting Nina's furrowed brow.

"You either don't have any Fritos or you've hidden them to keep me from ridiculing you."

Franco felt a rush of pleasure at the idea Nina remembered her penchant for Fritos. "Uh, Pop's making the fancy brisket chili tonight. I only put Fritos in his less fancy chuck stew meat version."

Nina laughed. "Forgive me. I didn't realize we were having the fancy version. What did I do to rate such extravagance?"

Franco reached for her hand, surprised when Nina didn't pull away. "You've always rated the good stuff. I'm sorry I didn't always give you what you deserve."

And just like that, the spell was back. For a moment, everything else in the room, in the world, fell away and they were simply two people, standing face-to-face, completely consumed by the magnetic pull of an attraction that had survived far longer than she'd ever hoped it could. The warmth of Nina's hands, the curve of her lips, the tenderness in her eyes—every detail about her was exactly as Franco remembered and she craved a return to the past to rectify her mistakes, to show Nina she was a better person than she'd been because no matter how altruistic her motives might have been for breaking things off, she knew now that it had been unforgivable not to let Nina make her own choice about their future.

"That was a long time ago," Nina said. "I'm sure we're both very different people now."

"I suppose that's true. Partly, anyway." Franco looked down at their clasped hands. "Do you think you could ever give me another chance?"

Nina's eyes fluttered shut for a moment and when she opened them, her gaze was firmly trained on the floor. "Franco, what are you doing?"

"Look, I didn't come here to try to insert myself back into your life. Hell, I didn't even know you were working at the courthouse, let alone the judge in Devon's case. And I sure didn't know that Jenna had tried to make a move on you after she encouraged me to bow out of your life." She squeezed Nina's hands. "But you have to admit there are a lot of coincidences here. Maybe the universe is trying to tell us something."

"The universe has a funny way of doing it." Nina slipped

her hands out of Franco's grasp and stepped back. "It's too late, Franco. I've moved on."

"Oh." Franco shoved her hands in her pockets, while she chewed on Nina's proclamation. She'd moved on. Of course she had. She was smart and funny and beautiful, inside and out. The very idea Nina would be available and open to any overture from her after all these years was ludicrous, and she'd been crazy to even entertain the idea. "Okay."

Nina placed a hand on the side of her face and gazed deep into her eyes. "There's a part of me that will always love you, but we can't reinvent the past."

Franco wanted to argue. To ask her how she knew with absolute certainty that they couldn't recapture some of the spark they'd had in their youth. Yes, they were different people now, but did different have to be an insurmountable obstacle to reconnecting? But Nina had been very clear that she wasn't interested in anything more, and even after all these years, she knew that pushing the point would only cause her to back completely away.

Pop chose that moment to stick his head in the door. "All good out here. You girls ready for dinner?"

A few minutes later, they were out on the deck, enjoying the chili and the cool night air. Nina sat right up next to the patio heater Franco had set up after she'd finished staining the deck and remarked several times about how cozy the patio was.

"Frances did all the work. She's been working herself silly since she came home to live. I'm lucky to have her."

He reached over and gripped her shoulder and gave it a tight squeeze, and she quickly changed the subject to keep from tearing up at the sentiment. "Working with my hands is a nice change of pace from arguing with people for a living."

"I bet," Nina said. "I used to have hobbies before I decided it would be a good idea to become a judge. Between running my docket and running for office, I barely have time to cook a meal." She lifted the last spoonful of chili from her bowl. "Which is why this meal is the highlight of my week. Thank you both."

Franco stacked the bowls and moved them to the side, but they lingered on the deck long after dinner, listening to Pop tell stories about her childhood. Nina laughed in all the right places, never giving a hint she'd heard them all before. For all she knew, Nina had long forgotten the details if she even remembered the stories at all.

It was almost ten when Nina said she needed to go and Franco walked her outside, lingering at her car, not ready for the night to end. "Tonight was nice. It was more than nice. It felt like old times." Franco hadn't meant to reference the past, but she couldn't help but wonder if Nina felt it too. But Nina's response caught her off guard.

"Tell me why you broke up with me," Nina asked. "I know it had to be more than Jenna telling you to. You always kept your own counsel. Was it something I did?"

"No, it had nothing to do with you." A tiny lie. "What difference does it make now? You've said you moved on."

Nina placed a hand on her heart. "You broke my heart, Franco. Yes, I've moved on, and no, I don't want to go back to what we had, but I would like to be your friend, and the only way I can see that happening is if we heal the past."

Franco glanced back toward the house. Pop was likely already sound asleep and snoring in his recliner. He was the only one who knew the truth, but did he even remember? Surely the statute of limitations had passed on her keeping his secrets. She sighed. Nina deserved to know the truth,+ and there would never be a perfect time to tell her. She motioned to the car. "Let's sit in there and I'll tell you."

CHAPTER THIRTEEN

Nina unlocked the car and climbed into the front seat. She wasn't entirely sure she wanted to hear what Franco was going to say, but she'd asked, so there was no turning back now. It was warm inside the car, but not nearly as warm as when she'd been sitting with Pop and Franco on the deck, eating chili, drinking beer, and reminiscing, and she knew the warmth she'd felt earlier had nothing to do with the temperature outside and everything to do with the feeling that she'd stepped back in time.

But she hadn't. It had been almost two decades since Franco had walked away from her, and no amount of pretending nothing had happened between them would rectify the pain she'd felt at being cut out of Franco's life. All these years, she'd had trouble trusting that any relationship would last, that any adversity was a team sport. She didn't need a therapist to tell her that her loneliness was the direct result of walling herself off from potentially getting hurt again, but she was ready to move past the pain of the past, and maybe this conversation would give her the closure she hadn't realized she desperately needed.

They sat for a few minutes in silence before Franco finally cleared her throat and started talking. "Freshman year. When they finally diagnosed Mom's cancer. It was advanced. More advanced than I ever told you."

Franco abruptly stopped the staccato sentences, and Nina wasn't sure how to react. Nineteen-year-old her wanted to pull Franco into her arms and tell her it would be okay, but the thirty-eight-year-old version was braced for whatever hammer Franco intended to drop next. She nodded, willing Franco to take the sign she should continue and thankfully, she did.

"She wanted to pretend she was okay. She didn't want Pop to worry, and she wanted me to enjoy freshman year and not feel obligated to take care of her."

"She loved you both. Very much."

Franco looked up and Nina almost melted at the tears in her eyes. Almost.

"The bills started piling up. Just a few more treatments, the doctors said. They referred us to one facility and then another, with each one promising they had the solution to cure the cancer, curb it, or at the very least mitigate her pain. Mom and Pop fell behind on the house payments, and they could barely pay utilities and groceries. They were completely underwater and at a loss about what to do."

"Why didn't you tell me all this?"

"I didn't know. Not at first."

Nina waited, bracing for whatever Franco might say next, but she was completely unprepared for her next words.

"Pop stole the drugs. He boosted the key right after his shift at the store and came back later when he knew the store would be busy, claiming he left his checkbook in his locker. He'd scoped out where the cameras were, and he knew exactly how to get around them. We were only in the store for five minutes, tops."

"Wait." Nina sat with her hand up while she ran through the gamut of thoughts crowding her mind. "I don't get it. Why would he do that? And how did you get involved? Hold on, you said 'we were only in the store for five minutes.' Were you in on it?"

"No." Franco's voice was a growl of indignation. "If I'd had any idea that's what he was doing, I never would've let it happen. I didn't find out until the police called him for questioning."

"How did they figure it was him?"

"Because out of all of the other employees who'd been at the store that day, he was the only one with a record." She paused and took a deep breath. "He had a conviction from back when he was nineteen. Drug possession—another thing I learned about after the fact. You can see how they'd focus on him as the employee most likely to have stolen the drugs."

"How did he even get a job working in a drug store with his record?"

Franco raised her eyebrows. "How do you think? After he'd applied for seven other jobs where he proactively explained in tedious detail the specifics of his background, he decided he needed to change his strategy. He lied on his application, and they were desperate for employees at the time, so they didn't run a thorough check. He'd worked at the store so long, he never imagined it would come up again."

Nina nodded, more to show she was following along than she agreed with Pop's strategy. She wanted to let Franco tell the story in her own way, but she had a burning question she needed her to answer. "Why do you think he took you with him that day?"

"Honestly, I think he didn't want to. It was a Saturday and you and Jenna were studying for finals. I spent the day with Mom and Pop. Later in the day, Pop said he had to run to the store and I told him I wanted to go too. He tried to talk me out of it, but I didn't understand why it was such a big deal for me to tag along. I figured out later, he was trying to keep me out of trouble."

"Well, I guess that didn't work out so well, did it?"

Regret flashed in Franco's eyes, and Nina instantly regretted the harsh words. "I'm sorry. That wasn't fair, but can you tell me how you wound up taking the blame for what he did?" Nina couldn't help but glance over at the house. Was Pop still snoring in his recliner? How could the kind and gentle man she'd known for so many years be the kind of person who would steal from his employer, let alone steal drugs to sell on the black market?

She shook away the thought. She saw similar situations all the time in her court. Seemingly together people who fell on hard times and opted for an illegal act they thought would have little impact on the alleged victim, which in this case was a big-name retailer. She often showed mercy for these strangers, so why was she resistant to forgive when it came to the dear man who'd just made her dinner and was more welcoming to her than her own parents had ever been?

Because whatever had happened that day had changed the course of her life and Franco's, through no fault of their own. Still, she needed to hear the rest of this painful story if she wanted any sense of closure. "Tell me what happened next."

Franco shrugged. "The store was pushing for the police to arrest Pop. They wanted him to do time to set an example. With Mom sick and the bills piling up, they couldn't afford a lawyer, and I didn't know anything about the legal system then. All I knew was that even with scholarships, my college expenses were only adding to the problem. If Pop went to jail, who would take care of Mom? Make sure she got the treatment she needed? Make sure the lights stayed on?"

She hung her head. "I went to the cops. Told them it was

me. I figured a National Merit Scholar had a good chance at getting probation. I got a deferred sentence, and after I completed my probation, the DA's office dismissed the case. I lost my scholarship and I had to answer lots of questions when I applied to U of H and Rice, but Pop stayed out of the system, and he was holding Mom in his arms when she died."

Nina wanted to grab her by the shoulders and shout "I lost out too," but hearing Franco's voice crack as she talked about her mother crushed her, and she shelved her personal loss for now to let Franco be with her own grief. She moved closer and took Franco in her arms. "I'm so sorry. She was a force."

Franco sank into her embrace. "She was. I would've done anything to make her life more comfortable. I miss her every day."

Nina held her tightly and searched for the right thing to say, but every option that sprang to mind was only an insensitive reminder of what she herself had lost. How was it possible that Franco had thought her only option was taking her father's place? Franco's family might not have had the means to hire a good lawyer, but she had. If only Franco had told her the truth. She could have gotten the money from her parents.

What would she have said to them? *My girlfriend, who you don't approve of anyway because she doesn't have the right name, house, pedigree, etc., needs money for a lawyer because her dad stole drugs from his employer to sell on the black market.* They wouldn't have cared about his motivation, only the result that might tarnish their own reputation and that of their precious only daughter. Franco had always been proud of what she'd accomplished, and to be colored with the brush of what her father had done and to have to beg for assistance from people she knew didn't like her would have been a nonstarter.

But why didn't she trust Nina enough to at least tell her what was happening? That was a question she needed answered. "I would've helped you."

Franco pulled back slightly, enough to look into her eyes. "I know. But it wasn't my story to tell. My parents loved you. They thought you were the best thing that could've ever happened to me. If you'd known what happened, it would've tainted your every interaction with them. Pop is proud, and I couldn't do that to him or you." She offered a half smile. "And I turned out okay. I did half my probation while helping Pop get his own handyman business up and going. After Mom died, I moved to Houston and enrolled at U of H."

"You didn't want to come back to Richards?"

"It was too weird. You and Jenna had moved on with your lives."

"That was your choice."

"Look, I hate how she did it, but Jenna was right when she told me it would be better for you if I walked away. You didn't need to be swept up into my drama. Besides, Richards pulled my scholarship. I could've appealed, but I needed a fresh start. U of H had a special program for people like me that was perfect. I had to work my ass off through school, but I earned every hour of that degree." She sighed. "Getting out of town was the best thing for me. I love Pop, but every time I saw him it was a reminder of what we'd both lost, and there were too many other memories here for me to be able to move on with my life."

Nina didn't have to ask what those other memories were. She'd experienced firsthand the trauma of waking up every day in a world where the biggest part that had kept her going had disappeared. She'd had to relearn how to make her way through the world, and it hadn't been easy. She could only imagine how hard it had been for Franco. *If only we'd been able to have each other.* "I would've helped you through all of it. Even if you hadn't told me the truth about what happened. I would've stood by your side. We could have figured it out—the court case, your mother's treatment—whatever needed to be done. Did you not trust me enough to come to me about this?" She paused, wavering about whether to ask the one question she really wanted to, ultimately deciding she had nothing to lose anymore. "Did you ever even love me?"

Franco pulled her close and wrapped her tightly in her arms. For a moment, Nina was lost in the warmth and familiarity of her embrace. She tucked her head under Franco's chin and let the flood of feelings from her past crest over them both. This was real, and in this moment she felt she was right where she belonged.

"Do you think we'll always be in love?"

Franco grabbed her hand and pulled her close. They'd gone for a walk after eating too much ice cream after dinner in the dorm cafeteria. It was still warm outside, the lingering vestiges of a too hot summer, but the real warmth Nina felt came when Franco whispered in her ear.

"I have absolutely no doubt." Franco left a trail of tender kisses along her ear and down her neck. "What would compel you to ask such a question?"

"I don't know. I guess I don't know anyone other than your parents who got together when they were young and managed to make it last."

"I guess it doesn't help that your parents aren't big fans of mine."

"They don't understand anyone who doesn't run in their absurdly exclusive social set. Trust me, you're not missing anything. You definitely won in the family department. I love your parents."

"And they love you, but not as much as I do." Franco placed a hand on either side of her face. "And I'm going to love you forever. I promise."

But the promise was a lie. Nina eased out of Franco's embrace, determined not to be tricked into believing otherwise. She didn't belong here. Nothing had changed. She and Franco had lived a charmed life. High school sweethearts headed off to college together with a full future already planned out. They had been young and naive, but she was neither now. When she found true love again, if it even existed, it wouldn't be based on dreams, but concrete realities. And the attraction and affection she felt for Franco right now? It wasn't real. It couldn't be. The only thing she could do was leave and refuse to repeat the past.

CHAPTER FOURTEEN

I don't understand why he's not getting a bond hearing."
Franco motioned for Jenna to follow her down the
hall. Jenna had wanted to meet somewhere other than the
courthouse, but she'd refused her request in order to make sure
that the first time she saw Jenna again after Nina's revelation
was a place she was unlikely to lose her cool. As it was, she
was having a hard time being patient with Jenna's constant
stream of questions and second-guessing, and she had to force
herself to acknowledge any other parent would have just as
much anxiety under the circumstances.

Once they were away from the crowd outside the
courtroom, Franco filled Jenna in. "I don't think a bond hearing
is a good idea. Lacy's father will show up again, and because
of who he, is the press will be out in force. With a big crowd
watching and the potential to be the lead story on the evening
news, the prosecutor will feel like he has no choice but to go
all out to make sure the bond doesn't get reduced.

"I'm going to meet with the ADA today to pick up a copy
of the evidence they have so far, and I'll see if we can come
to some kind of agreement about the bond amount, without
journalists lurking nearby. Once I've had an opportunity to
review the evidence, I'll discuss it with Devon."

"What about me? Don't I have a right to know?"

Franco seethed at the question, which completely deflated her attempt at staying professional. "We don't all get to know everything we think we should. Like for instance, were you ever going to tell me that the reason you suggested I break up with Nina was so you would be free to make your move?"

Jenna's face went completely white, and her eyes darted like she was looking for the nearest exit.

"Don't try to deny it," Franco said. "Nina told me everything."

Jenna's eyes narrowed. "You talked to her? When?"

Now she wished she'd kept her feelings in check. She didn't want to admit she'd seen Nina personally, certain that Jenna would try to twist that to Devon's advantage. "What difference does it make? It's true, right?"

"Not the way you make it sound. Yes, I had a thing for Nina, but I would've thought it was a bad idea for her to be with a drug dealer who was dropping out of college, even if I was someone who'd just met her on the street."

"We were friends. I trusted you. Valued your opinion. Because I had no idea you were biased. You were perfectly happy to have me out of the picture."

"Yes, we were friends, but Nina was the hub. Without her, you and I never would've been friends—we were too different. So, was I happy you were gone so I could have Nina to myself? Yes. Yes, I was."

"Little rich girl, always getting what she wants."

"You don't know anything about me. Besides, Nina rejected me, and she didn't even take a second to think about it before she did."

"Why did you even contact me to represent Devon if you thought I was such a loser?"

"I was wrong." Jenna gave an exasperated sigh. "Clearly.

Look at you. You're a big-shot lawyer. Nina's a judge. Me? I'm the girl who went to a party after the girl I lusted over rejected me and slept with the first drunk frat boy I found only to get pregnant and have my parents toss me out of the family. I never finished my degree and I work as a receptionist." She put her hands on her hips in a display of defiance. "You win. Are you happy?"

Franco didn't answer right away, her mind spinning through the revelations Jenna had just thrown her way. What Jenna described was rough, but it didn't excuse her behavior, then or now. "I'm not the kind of person who takes pleasure in another person's unhappiness. And to be perfectly clear, neither of us won, Jenna."

Jenna hung her head. "I know. I'm sorry I implied otherwise. I was stupid. I created this fantasy in my head where Nina would come running to me, but Nina was only ever in love with you. I was a fool. A pregnant college dropout kind of fool."

Franco looked carefully at Jenna's face, and the abject remorse she saw there confirmed her gut reaction. Jenna really was sorry and nothing she could say could make her feel any worse about what she'd done. "It took a lot of courage to have a baby on your own. Wait, sorry. I just assumed…" Now it was Franco's turn to feel like a fool.

"It's okay. You may think I'm awful, but I never told the guy about Devon. I only ever knew his first name, and sure I could've tried harder to find out more, but the idea of dealing with the aftermath of my poor decisions with a total stranger was inconceivable." She let out a mirthless laugh. "Perfect word for it, wouldn't you say?"

"I'm sorry you had to go through a pregnancy, raise a son on your own."

"I'm not. Raising Devon has been the only thoroughly

good thing I've ever done. He's smart and kind and honest." She took a breath and stared hard at Franco with tears in her eyes. "Which is why I know he didn't kill Lacy. He cared deeply for her, and he would've done anything for her. The police need to be focused on the Sig Ep brothers who were at the party that night. Talk about spoiled rich kids who think they can get away with anything."

Her words triggered Franco's memory. "I've been meaning to ask you. How did Devon afford to pledge, let alone live in the house?"

"Don't look at me. I only supported his idea about pledging because I knew it would give him contacts he could use to be successful later in life. Lacy's dad footed the bill. Said he wanted Devon to have the full experience like he'd had. He even set him up in the house as a pledge, which is unheard of."

"Whoa, Harry Benton is a legacy?"

"Big time. Devon says they have a huge plaque with his name on it at the house and he funds three different scholarships they offer. I think he supported Devon because he didn't want his Panhellenic daughter dating some nobody."

Now it made sense why none of Devon's fraternity brothers had offered anything more than a passing comment by way of support. "Do you know the other guys in the fraternity?"

"Only by name."

"Make me a list. Get me any contact information you have. Did Devon have his phone on him when he was arrested?"

"No, I have it. It was in his things when I went to pick up his stuff from the house."

"Great. Start going through it. Nothing is off-limits."

"Besides phone numbers for frat boys, what am I looking for?"

"Anything that might be even remotely related to this case. Photos showing Devon and Lacy, smiling and laughing, with friends, with each other—you get the idea. Anything to support the idea it's ludicrous to think he would hurt her." Franco considered how to word what she wanted to say next. Hell, she should just spit it out. "If you find something incriminating, I need to see that too."

"There won't be anything."

"Good. But just in case, I'm putting you on notice that if you try to hide what you find, the truth will come out. It's entirely possible that Harry Benton has already seen everything on that phone if it was at the house for any length of time before you got it. If there was something implicating Devon, true or not, the DA's office may have it already, and that might explain why they've been playing hardball on the bond."

"Fine," Jenna said. "I'll let you know what I find. When are you going to meet with the prosecutor?"

Franco looked at her watch. "I should go now."

"Call me later? After you meet with Devon?"

She didn't want to be locked into anything, but she got it. Jenna would worry until she knew what actual evidence the police had and what Devon had to say about it. Franco needed to tell Jenna it wouldn't matter what she found out unless Devon gave her permission to talk to his mom about it, but she'd dealt enough blows today. "I'll definitely call you," she said, satisfied with the vague commitment.

She turned to go and froze in place at the sight of Nina passing not three feet from them. They hadn't spoken since Friday night when, after she'd bared her soul, Nina had abruptly ended their talk and driven away. Against her better judgment, she'd sent Nina several texts over the weekend, but given up after her overtures were met with silence. She wasn't sure what she'd expected, but she'd held out hope that telling Nina the whole story would allow them to find their way past their nineteen-year rift and into friendship at the very least. If the look on Nina's face right now was any indication, she'd been naive to think their relationship had healed.

"Good morning, Judge."

"Good morning, Ms. Rossi."

Franco felt a not so gentle nudge from behind and looked over her shoulder to see Jenna standing practically on top of her. She shot her a blistering look and turned back to Nina and continued the charade of professional civility. "I was headed to your courtroom to talk to the prosecutor on Devon Grant's case. Are you going to be in chambers later this morning?"

A look of surprise crossed Nina's face, and she looked around like she was checking to see if anyone else was watching their exchange. "As I explained to you, last week, Ms. Rossi, if you would like to discuss the disposition of a particular case, you will need to file the appropriate motions and request a hearing where both sides can appear to present their case." She shot a pointed look at Jenna. "Otherwise, we have nothing to discuss. Am I making myself clear?"

Franco willed Jenna to keep her mouth shut and nodded. "Perfectly. I'll be sure to make sure I loop the prosecutor in on anything I need to discuss with you."

She grinned at the quick flash of fear in Nina's eyes, waved good-bye to Jenna, and walked away from them both. She had a tinge of guilt about her comment, but if Nina was going to insist they couldn't have any conversations outside the presence of others, then she deserved to squirm a little at the idea she might talk about their personal lives in the presence of strangers. Not that she would. It wasn't like she wanted her personal life on display either, but she wasn't done trying to reconcile with Nina. Not by a long shot.

❖

Judge Keene's door was open, but he was engrossed in whatever was displayed on his computer monitor, so Nina knocked on the doorframe to get his attention.

"Hi, Nina," he said, barely looking up. "Come in here and save me from the woes of this budget."

She took a seat across from his desk and crossed her legs. "Tell me about it. Doing my part was hard enough, I don't even want to think about having to compile the numbers for all of the courts."

"The trials of being chief." He typed rapidly for a moment, and then pushed the keyboard away and folded his hands on the desktop. "I was half expecting you wanted to meet to ask for an extension on getting your numbers to me, but Lois said you turned them in Friday. Bless you for that. What's up?"

She twisted her hands in her lap for a moment while she sorted out exactly what to say. Up until the moment she'd run into Franco and Jenna in the hallway, she'd been questioning the wisdom of requesting this meeting, but seeing them both at the courthouse only solidified her resolve. "I need you to reassign a case."

His brow furrowed and he leaned back in his chair. "I don't think you've ever asked me to reassign a case in the entire time you've been on the bench."

"And I wouldn't now if I didn't think it was the right thing to do."

"I get that. Can you tell me a little more?"

"It's the Devon Grant case," she said. A beat passed, and when he didn't show any sign of recognition, she added, "He's accused of killing Lacy Benton. Harry Benton's daughter."

"Oh, right. That's a big one. It's still early stages, right?"

"True, but a few things have come to light that could affect my impartiality on the case."

"Is that so."

Now he was leaning forward, like he was hanging on her every word, which only made her want to tell him never mind and get out of there as fast as she could. But she was here, and she truly believed she had to give him full disclosure. She cleared her throat. "What I'm about to tell you is personal and I'd appreciate it if no one else knew unless it's absolutely necessary."

"Fire away."

"I used to date the defense attorney. More than date. We were in a long-term committed relationship."

"Okay. Anything else?"

She'd expected more—shock, surprise, something—but he looked like she'd told him a piece of year-old gossip. He couldn't already know, could he? No, she was being paranoid. He was probably just waiting to hear the full scope of her confession before he reacted. "Yes. I used to be very good friends with the defendant's mother. We had a bitter falling-out." She stopped talking and waited for him to respond.

"Do you know the defendant?"

"No. His mother and I parted ways long before he was born."

He looked puzzled. "Wait, isn't he twenty years old?"

"Nineteen."

"I find it hard to believe you would let a relationship and a friendship breakup from almost twenty years ago impede you from being fair to all parties. Truth is, I'd find it hard to believe a breakup from last week would have any impact on your judgment. You're one of the most honest people I know."

Normally, she'd appreciate the compliment, but he wasn't getting it. "Honesty is what has me sitting here in front of you in the first place. I honestly don't know if I can set aside my feelings."

He waved his arm in a dismissive, no big deal kind of

way. "Think about all of the times some potential juror has held up their hand and said they didn't think they could be fair. What do we do?"

She replayed the last jury selection in her courtroom and recalled grilling a juror to get him to admit he could set aside his bias and follow the law. She never liked to think of it as bullying, but it could definitely be perceived that way, but it was absolutely necessary, or the entire panel would get the hint and start making excuses of why they couldn't serve. "I hear you, but I'm not some random person, trying to get out of jury duty."

"No, you're not. Which means you're uniquely qualified to compartmentalize your feelings in favor of the facts, and I have every confidence you can and will do so. Don't worry about Harry Benton and the press and the election. Do what's right and everything will work out. Besides, Larabee should be back soon, and you won't have to worry about this case or any of the others you've been babysitting."

She wanted to press the point, but he was already back to staring at his monitor and grunting about the budget. She murmured a quiet thanks, leaving silent the "for nothing" part she was feeling, and showed herself out of the room, praying Larabee's recovery came soon because the idea of facing Franco in her courtroom was more than she could handle.

CHAPTER FIFTEEN

Franco walked into the DA workroom and took a moment to
assess. It was a tiny room with a desk on either side of the
entrance. A harried-looking prosecutor sat behind each of the
piled high desks, and several defense attorneys were crowded
into the rest of the space. Not much different than the Harris
County courthouse. She glanced at the door toward the back
of the room, which she suspected was the chief prosecutor's
office. "Is Rigley in there?" she asked a man standing to her
right.

"Yep." He stuck out his hand. "Lyle Evans. I don't think
I've seen you around here before. You new?"

Franco sized him up and decided he was simply being
friendly. She gripped his hand. "Franco Rossi. My main office
is in Harris County."

"What brings you to Dallas?"

She settled on the least complicated answer to the loaded
question. "Checking on a case for an old friend." She pointed
at the door again. "Has he been in there with the door shut for
long?"

Lyle shrugged. "I just got here myself. I'd go ahead and
knock if it were me. He'll probably forget he shut it and it's a
no-jury day, so he could stay in there all day."

"Thanks." Franco strode the four steps to the door and gave it a solid rap.

"Come in."

She pushed the door open to find a nice-looking dark-haired guy sitting behind a desk that took up most of the space. Unlike the prosecutors sitting outside his door, he looked calm and relaxed with his jacket off and his tie loose. She imagined it was much easier to find your Zen when you didn't have defense attorneys sitting on the edge of your desk, clamoring for attention. "Mr. Rigley?"

He laughed. "You lookin' for my dad?" He stuck out a hand. "Name's Johnny—no mister necessary. What can I do for you?"

She smiled, unable to resist his good-natured manner. "I'm Franco. I came in to talk to you about Devon Grant." She watched, waiting for the smile to disappear, but it didn't despite his next words.

"That guy's in a world of hurt. Found the poor girl's blood on his clothes, and I hear they had a fight right before she went missing. You here to try and work out a deal? Because I'll need to run any deals by her family before I can sign off."

She motioned to the chair across from his desk. "Mind if I sit?"

"Help yourself."

She settled into the chair. "I was hoping we could start from the beginning. Before I was hired on, one of the public defenders requested a bond hearing, and of course that was delayed after the shooting. I thought we could come to an agreement about the bond and not bother setting a new hearing."

"No can do. I've got strict instructions from my boss that Grant's bond isn't getting reduced unless the judge sees fit to do it on her own."

"Who's your boss?"

"Lennox Roy. She used to be the chief in here, but now she's the new super chief."

Lennox. Nina's best friend. Who'd already made it perfectly clear she wasn't a fan. "The kid's local and so is his mother. She hired me and she'll be the surety on the bond. Do you really think she's going to let him skip out on her obligation?"

"Seen it happen. A man in a corner will bite whoever he needs when he's desperate to break free."

He wasn't wrong, but Franco knew in her soul Devon wasn't the type to run and hide. "Okay, but like I said, he's a kid, not a man, and he's scared to death. I think he's more likely to whimper in the corner than do any biting."

"Just the same, I'd rather be cautious."

"You getting a lot of pressure from Harry Benton?"

"You implying I take my lead from the victim's family?"

Franco noted his voice took on a slight edge for the first time since they'd started talking. "Not trying to imply anything other than I'm sure you're juggling a lot on this one." She watched his face and was certain she noted a slight nod. "I get it. I'm just doing my job and making sure I cover all the angles. If we need to request another bond hearing, that's the route we'll take. Can I go ahead and pick up the discovery?"

Johnny's wide smile was back, and he reached across his desk and pulled a folder out of a bin on a nearby shelf. "It's all here and ready for you. You're not going to find much more in there. Guy was drinking, argued with his girlfriend, blacked out. When he woke up his girlfriend was missing and he's wearing her blood. Not sure how they handle things in Harris County, but up here those facts make for a pretty tight case."

She wasn't sure whether he was taunting her or whether he was simply a super friendly guy even when discussing murder.

She tucked the folder under her arm and started toward the door. She was one step out of his office, when she decided to gamble on Johnny Rigley's nice demeanor. She turned to face him and hoped she looked friendly too. "Throw me a bone."

"Anything specific?"

"What was his motive?"

Johnny shrugged. "Who knows. Kegger gone wrong. Maybe she looked the wrong way at another guy. Could've been anything."

"True. True." She waved and started back toward the door, but she paused again just before leaving. "Or maybe he didn't do it."

Back out in the hall, Franco contemplated her next move. She wanted to dig into the discovery right there, but the options for spreading out a bunch of papers were slim. She was scouting out a solution when she heard someone call her name. It was the woman who'd been with Nina at the hospital the night of the shooting.

"Hi, you're Franco, right?"

"I am, and I'm embarrassed to admit I don't remember your name."

"Wren Bishop. And I'm not surprised you don't remember. There was kind of a lot going on when we met." She stuck her hand out and Franco grasped it. Wren was as much of a fashion plate as Nina—no wonder they were friends.

"Are you a prosecutor?"

Wren laughed. "Hardly. I work for the PD's office."

"Ah, then you know your way around this place. Any chance you could tell me if there's anywhere I can hole up for a bit and review some documents?"

"I know the perfect place." Wren started walking and motioned for her to follow. A few flights of stairs later, they emerged on the ninth floor into a much quieter space than the floors down below. Wren led them into a suite and into an office even smaller than Rigley's.

"Have a seat," Wren said. "Coffee?"

Franco almost forget to answer in her fascination with the activity happening behind Wren's desk. She was pulling things out of a tiny refrigerator, pouring water into an electric kettle, and spooning coffee from a bag with a fancy label into a French press. "You've got quite the setup going on here."

"What can I say? I like coffee, and what they serve everywhere else in the building doesn't pass muster."

"Thanks for the warning." Franco took the mug Wren handed her and took a sip. "This is amazing."

"I know, right? I wish I could take credit, but all I do is heat, pour, and plunge. These are definitely magical beans."

Franco took another sip and looked around Wren's office. "I appreciate the coffee and all, but this place is a little small for one person, let alone two."

Wren pushed everything on her desk to the side. "Sure, if we were working on different things." She pointed at the files Franco had in her lap. "I just wrapped up a big case and I need a distraction. That's the discovery in the Grant case, right?"

Franco hesitated, unsure where Wren was headed. "Uh, yes."

"Can I look at it with you? We can even talk it through. I mean, chances are good I know more about the local players than you do considering you're from out of town." She gave Franco an earnest, pleading look. "Don't worry. I'm not going to ask you for any confidential information about your client, but why not let another lawyer who is likely to believe he's innocent before being proved guilty give you another set of eyes."

Franco couldn't argue with the logic. She didn't know Wren, but she was a friend of Nina's, and that had to mean she was an honorable person. Also, the fact that she was a friend of Nina's meant there was a slight chance that while Wren was helping her out, she might find a way to get something in return.

They spent the next hour poring over the police report and evidence.

"They didn't recover a weapon," Wren observed. "But the coroner says the wound appeared to be the result of a cut from a regular ol' steak knife."

"Not many cold-blooded killers running around with steak knives, I imagine."

"Precisely," Wren said. "This was a crime of passion, and the killer took advantage of whatever weapon was nearby."

"You realize that logic doesn't bode well for my client. You know, the boyfriend."

"Oops." Wren smiled. "Well, there are lots of possible sources of passion."

"True. I need to talk to Devon's fraternity brothers to see who else Lacy might have interacted with that night."

"You need an investigator."

"Are you offering yourself for the role?"

"No, but I can give you some recommendations."

"That would be great."

"And I'm also inviting you to dinner."

Franco was certain she looked shocked because Wren immediately followed her invitation with "With friends. Well, my girlfriend and one of our friends. But we're all friends. Say you'll come."

She nodded, not entirely sure what she'd just agreed to but not wanting to be responsible for deflating Wren's cheerful demeanor. Besides, she could use a break from babysitting Pop. "I'll be there."

Chapter Sixteen

Nina shifted the bottle of wine to one hand and pressed the elevator button for the top floor. Her parents lived in a posh building like this one, but in New York, not Dallas, and it had been a long time since she'd lived in the manner they'd tried so hard to get her to become accustomed to.

Not that she begrudged anyone else living in a building with a doorman and private access to the top floor, but it wasn't for her. Too many memories of how much her parents' heavy-handed influence was associated with an extravagant lifestyle led her to resist the trappings of her youth. Wren, on the other hand, had a great relationship with her parents, who happened to own this building as part of their massive real estate portfolio.

When the elevator stopped, she stepped out and strode toward the only door on the right and rang the bell. When the door swung open, she nearly dropped the wine when she realized she was face-to-face with Franco.

"What are you doing here?"

"I could ask the same thing," Franco said. She looked back over her shoulder. "Wren invited me. I didn't realize Lennox was her girlfriend until I showed up." She lowered her voice to a whisper. "They know, don't they?"

"Know what?" Nina asked.

Franco waved her hand back and forth between them. "About us. That we were…"

"Kind of hard to finish that sentence, isn't it?"

"Not really. Not for me."

Nina partly wanted to press the point, get Franco to say out loud exactly what she'd call whatever they had between them, but other parts of her wanted to get back in the elevator and get the hell out of here. She had no idea what had possessed Wren to invite Franco over, but she knew for certain sharing dinner with Franco and her friends at the same time was going to be like walking through a minefield. She was still assessing her options when Lennox appeared behind Franco with a worried look on her face.

"You're here," Lennox said.

"Why yes, I am. And I'm not the only one, apparently." Nina hoped her expression told Lennox exactly how much she wasn't enjoying the surprise guest. Just in case, she grabbed Lennox's arm and pointed to the hallway on the right. "I need you to show me that new furniture Wren bought for the guest bedroom because I'm thinking about redoing my place. Come on."

A moment later, she was standing with Lennox inside one of the guest rooms with the door shut. "What's she doing here?"

"Wren invited her."

"I got that much. I love your girlfriend, but what was she thinking?"

"You know Wren, always looking out for the underdog. She ran into Franco at the courthouse and helped her out with some questions she had about how things work in our neck of the woods. Then she invited her for dinner. I had no idea she was coming, and I wasn't happy when I found out. She got here about thirty minutes ago, and Wren's already roped her into looking at the file on Daniel's case. Believe it or not, she has some good ideas."

"Et tu, Lennox?" Nina sank down on the edge of the bed. "I should go."

Lennox sat down beside her. "No, you shouldn't."

"She filed an appearance in the Devon Grant case. She's going to appear in my court."

"As have I and Wren and a ton of other people you've shared meals with over the years."

"You sound just like Keene."

"Well, he's right. It's impossible to work at the courthouse and not have some overlap between the personal and professional."

"Said the woman who, up until six months ago, had a no dating anyone at the courthouse rule."

"Are you planning to date her?"

"No, of course not." Nina heard the exaggerated growl in her own voice. "Not even in the plan."

"Great. Then you don't have a problem."

"I'm up for election. I have to think about how everything looks."

"Then you probably shouldn't have agreed to have dinner with Wren and me. Seriously, I don't think the small number of Dallas County voters who will turn out for an off-year election are going to count a dinner with friends against you. And if you think your mentee, Johnny Rigley, is going to call your character into question, then you're crazy." She stood and reached for Nina's hand. "I made an amazing dinner and I expect you to stay and eat it. If you're still uncomfortable after the main course, you can leave before dessert."

Nina took Lennox's hand and stood. "What's for dessert?"

"You'll have to stick around to find out. But, Nina?"

"Yes?"

"You're going to want to stick around."

The door to the guest room opened and Wren stuck her head in. "Uh, this is getting a little awkward. Are you two going to hide out in here all night?"

Nina stuck her tongue out at her. "I was thinking about it. I'm not sure what the proper protocol is when your best friend's girlfriend invites your long-lost lover over to dinner."

Wren lifted her shoulders. "I'm not going to lie, I knew the lay of the land, but I invited her on a whim, mostly because she seemed like she needed some people while she's in town. I know what it's like when you're working in a new place and you don't have any people."

Lennox pointed at her. "See, I told you."

Nina remembered the stories Wren told her about when she'd started at the public defender's office. She'd received an icy reception from the other PDs who figured her background at a top tier big law firm in town meant she couldn't relate to the type of work they did or handle the caseload. Wren had proved them wrong and managed to make friends in the process, but it hadn't been easy. Of course she'd want to extend welcoming overtures to someone like Franco. Nina only wished Wren's hospitality didn't intrude on her personal life.

But Franco was here and she was here, and dinner smelled good, and leaving now would be beyond rude. Plus, there was a tiny part of her that craved more contact with Franco, and what safer way to manage her emotions than to have the contact take place with her friends at her side. "Fine, but this is a dinner with friends, nothing more." She shook a finger at Wren. "If you're trying to play matchmaker, I will make you pay. Understood?"

Wren gave her a "who me?" look and held the door open

wide. As Nina walked through she offered up a silent prayer. *Just let me get through this with my heart intact.*

❖

Franco paced Wren and Lennox's living room for several minutes, but the activity did nothing to quell the tumbling in the pit of her stomach. She should leave. It was clear Nina had no idea she'd be here tonight, and she wasn't sure what to make about that fact. Had Wren made a conscious choice not to tell Nina? It wasn't like Wren had given her a heads-up either. For all she knew, Wren didn't know the details of their past, and why would she? Her relationship with Nina was so far in the past, most people would expect they both would've moved on by now. But she hadn't. Not really. Sure, there'd been other relationships, but she'd never managed to find anyone who captured her heart the way Nina had, and eventually she'd given up looking. She had a fulfilling career, and she'd always made sure her days were jam-packed with the career she loved. A lover, unless they were in the same line of work, wouldn't understand the focus and devotion she committed to her work, and if they were in the same field, they'd have their own distractions.

Nina would understand.

The thought was a nonstarter. Nina wasn't interested in any kind of relationship with her—she'd made that perfectly clear, and Franco couldn't blame her.

She glanced at the hallway where first Lennox and Nina, and then Wren had disappeared. She could follow their path and force her way into their tight-knit circle or she could make everyone more comfortable and leave. She was still weighing her options a second later when the three of them appeared and started walking toward her.

"Could I be a ruder hostess?" Wren asked with a perfect, perky smile that Franco was beginning to learn was her go-to expression. "Dinner will be ready in about ten minutes, but in the meantime, let's have cocktails. I'm having a dirty martini. What about the rest of you?"

"Same," Nina said. "Make mine a double, please."

This was it. Once she had a drink in her hand, she'd made a commitment to stick around. Franco looked over at Lennox, silently encouraging her to speak up next to give her a few extra seconds to make her decision.

"I've got some great local microbrews on hand if you're interested," Lennox said, as if she could read her mind.

The friendly overture sealed the deal. "Yeah," Franco said. "That sounds great."

Lennox and Wren disappeared to get drinks and deal with the last of the dinner prep, leaving her alone in the room with Nina. At first, she pretended to be absorbed in taking in every detail of the gorgeous space, but as the silence between them hovered, she was consumed with the desire to shatter the barrier. "If you want me to leave, I will."

"Do you want to leave?"

Franco took a moment to consider the question. "No, I don't. But I also don't want to intrude. Wren and Lennox are your friends, and I really didn't have any idea what I was walking into tonight. One word from you and I'm out of here." She paused for a moment while she thought of the exact thing she wanted to say. "I promise I'm not trying to make your life miserable, but if there's any way for us to land on friendship, I'd love the opportunity to make it happen. It may sound silly after all these years, but I miss you. I've always missed you, and if we could be friends at the very least, then I know my life would be better for it."

She stuck out her hand. "Friends it is."

Franco clasped her hand with a firm press, lingering for just a second before letting go. "Friends," she said with a big grin. She leaned closer to Nina. "So, as one friend to another, can I just say this place is amazing? Is Wren secretly an heiress?"

Nina laughed. "No secret about it. You've probably heard of her parents. They own Bishop Development."

Franco's eyes widened. "Of course I've heard of them. They're the biggest real estate developers in Houston, probably all of south Texas."

"I know. But you should know that Wren has plenty of money of her own. She worked at Dunley Thornton before she came to the PD's office."

"I'm guessing there's a story there."

"There is, and I'll let her tell it, but suffice it to say that she found her calling in public service, and I don't think she's ever going back."

Franco filed the fact away under reasons why she liked Wren. And if Wren was such a good person, then Lennox must be too. She wasn't looking to stay in Dallas any longer than she needed to get Pop's life back on track, but she'd be coming back and forth for Devon's case, and it would be nice to have some friends in town to meet up with when she did. She looked over at Nina, who staring intently her way. Friends. It wasn't the role she wanted Nina to play in her life, not the only one, anyway, but if it was all Nina would agree to, she'd take it because the idea of having nothing was too much to bear.

An hour later, they'd finished a delicious meal, and Wren and Lennox cleared their plates and returned to the table with fancy apple tarts and homemade vanilla ice cream. "I hope you saved room," Wren said, setting the first plate in front of Franco.

"I didn't, but that's not going to stop me because this looks incredible. Is the ice cream really homemade?"

"Everything's homemade," Lennox added. "Wren's not big on cooking, but she's recently started taking pastry classes, and all I can say is I'm glad you two are here to help eat all of this because I'm gaining a ton of weight as a result of her new hobby."

Franco dug into the dessert and moaned. "It's delicious."

Lennox and Nina chimed in with similar sentiments, and for the next few minutes the only sound in the room was that of their spoons clinking against the dessert bowls as they devoured the delicious food. When everyone professed they could eat no more, Wren posed a question to Franco.

"Is Harris County much different than Dallas?"

"Aside from the fact everyone there knows me? No, not much. I mean every place has its idiosyncrasies, but Dallas isn't a standout in that regard."

"When are you going back to Houston?"

Lennox's question was met with silence, and Nina spotted the subtle motion of Wren shoving her under the table. "Sorry, I meant how are you going to handle the case if you're back in Houston?"

If Franco was perturbed by the question, she didn't show it. "I've handled cases all over the state. Hasn't been a problem before to make the trip back for court settings. I plan to hire an investigator while I'm here and keep in touch with my client through them when I'm not in town."

"You can't go wrong with Skye Keaton as an investigator," Wren said. "She's not cheap, but well worth the price."

Franco shot a look at Nina, who was trying to act like she'd checked out of the conversation, but she could tell by the way she shifted slightly in her chair that the conversation was getting a little too close to the specifics of the case for her comfort. "I'll keep Skye in mind. Have you thought about using her for Daniel's case?"

Lennox pursed her lips and set her fork down like she'd just lost her appetite. "Did I say something wrong?" Franco asked.

"Skye's looking into it already," Wren said, "but so far she hasn't had any luck."

"Do you think she's not doing a good job?"

"I'm sure she means well, but I'd prefer to look into Daniel's case myself."

"And what will you do if you get a witness statement, and they contradict themselves on the stand? Get your brother's defense counsel to call you as a witness to impeach the witness? The jury will blow you off as being biased. Are you planning to serve as defense counsel too? Can you even do that while working for the DA's office? Have you even—" Franco caught herself before she could say more, certain that she'd just stepped over the line of what might be considered polite or even friendly dinner conversation, so she was surprised at Lennox's next words.

"Obviously, I haven't thought this through as well as I could have, but it's hard to trust anyone else with Daniel's case. Been there, done that."

"Didn't you say his case is in Tarrant County? A friend from law school works in the PD's office over there. If it's okay with you, I can reach out to him and see if he can rustle up any inside info. I trust him to be discreet."

"That would be great," Lennox said, shooting her a grateful smile.

Wren reached over and squeezed Lennox's hand, and Franco watched the tender exchange for a moment before glancing over to catch Nina doing the same. A second later, Nina looked up and met her gaze and she saw her own feelings of nostalgia reflected in her eyes. All these years later, she still remembered what it felt like to be in love the way Wren and Lennox were in love. How was that possible? The only suitable answer was their love had never died. But that couldn't be true. If it was, surely they would've found a way to make it work. *You walked away. Just because you ultimately found professional success, you didn't try hard enough to hold on to what you had with Nina. You don't deserve to have her be in love with you. Not anymore.*

Franco spent the rest of the evening putting on what she hoped was a good show of participating in the conversation while her mind was busy digging up all the examples of why the insurmountable rift between her and Nina was all her fault. It wasn't like she didn't already know that to be the case, but over the years, she'd glossed over the facts and applied a lens of "it wasn't meant to be, or it would've been" to their love story. By the end of the evening, she'd resolved to be happy with any attention Nina was willing to give, and hope that friendship was a possibility for the future.

She and Nina left at the same time, and the elevator ride to the first floor was silent. When they reached the lobby, Franco held open the door and let Nina walk through first. She handed her ticket to the valet but noticed Nina didn't do the same. "Where did you park?"

"I didn't drive." She smiled. "I've had Wren's martinis before, and since I had two to your one beer, I made a good decision." She held up her phone. "I'm going to call for a car."

"No way." Franco motioned to her car. "I'm sober and have wheels." She opened the passenger door and beckoned for Nina to get in. "Friends give each other rides. Like no big deal. Seriously." She mentally counted backward from five. If Nina didn't get in the car before she got to one, she would bow out gracefully, disappointed, but a little wiser about the boundaries of their new relationship.

Four, three, two...

"If you're sure you don't mind."

"Of course not." Franco held the door while Nina stepped inside. She reached down and caught the edge of Nina's jacket and tucked it up against her side. As she started to stand again, she met Nina's eyes, which were staring at her with a mixture of curiosity and a tinge of heat, and she was struck by the intimacy of the act. "Sorry about that. I didn't want it to get caught in the door. I promise, I wasn't trying to cross any friendship lines."

"It's okay, Franco. We're going to stumble a bit before we figure out our new normal."

"I guess that's true."

"I know it is, but I meant what I said about giving this a try."

Franco wished they'd done a better job at defining "this," but this wasn't the time or place to push any boundaries. In fact, she was committed to not pushing any boundaries at all. Yes, she wanted Nina back, as more than a friend, but if the sparks were to return, it would have to be Nina's decision, not hers. All those years ago, she'd walked away, but now she was going to stay right here no matter what adversity might happen and show Nina she was in this for the long haul. And if friendship was all she got in return, then she'd settle for whatever level of friendship Nina was willing to give. But she secretly held out hope there would be something more.

CHAPTER SEVENTEEN

Nina poured herself a cup of coffee and flipped through the Sunday paper, reading the final installment of the feature series about the Parks and Rec Killer. As a rule, she wasn't a big fan of reporters, but Macy Moran had knocked it out of the park with this story. If Lennox could see her right now, she'd give her a hard time about her choice of reading material, but delving into true crime wasn't just her occupation—it was one of her favorite hobbies. Like Wren, she'd started out working for a big, corporate law firm, but decided there wasn't enough money in the world to keep her tethered to clients who demanded she sacrifice every moment of her free time to keep their money and other assets protected. Applying to the DA's office was one of the best decisions she'd ever made, and winning a seat as a criminal court judge was a total bonus.

When she finished reading Moran's story, she fired up her laptop. She'd had Reggie scan Daniel Roy's file and upload it so she could review it over the weekend. This was her second time flipping through the pages, but nothing new jumped out. The facts were scarce and simple and odd.

Daniel Roy had been found unconscious in a drug house with a dead junkie in the next room and a gun with his fingerprints on it lying on the floor beside him. Daniel had a record, mostly lower-level drug arrests, but nothing violent.

He'd been charged with murder but had pled guilty early on in the case to twenty years in prison, half of which he'd have to serve before he was even eligible for parole. Lennox's big beef with the sentence was the fact her brother didn't remember a thing about the evening, but his defense attorney—Gloria Leland, Lennox's girlfriend at the time—had convinced him to accept the twenty-year offer.

She didn't blame Lennox for being angry about the outcome. Twenty years was a big stretch for a murder case with no witnesses and no motive, and when the defendant had no recollection of the crime, an offer of two decades' worth of time was downright ludicrous.

She made a few notes, but there wasn't much to go on. She was about to shut down her laptop and take a shower when her phone buzzed with a text.

This is your "friend" letting you know I found something I think might be yours when I was at the car wash this morning. Did Cinderella lose an earring?

She stared at Franco's text after instinctively reaching for her right ear for her favorite jade earrings. Of course, she wasn't wearing them now, but the message spurred her to get up and check her jewelry box. She'd been really tired the night before and didn't have any recollection of whether she'd made it home with all her bangles intact, but when she opened the box, there lay a lone jade teardrop. She spent a moment digging through the rest of her pieces, but she needn't have bothered since she was certain Franco had its twin.

Cinderella here. Pic please.

It took a moment, but when the photo loaded onto her phone, she recognized the earring right away. *Yep. That's mine, all right.*

Any chance you'd be up for lunch?

Nina tapped her fingers against the table, while she considered her response. Her first instinct was to say no. It was easier and cleaner to steer clear of spending any time alone with Franco. What if it was Lennox or Wren asking her to lunch, what then? The answer was easy. She'd go in a heartbeat, and never give the decision a second thought.

Nina stared at the text from Franco, wishing she had x-ray vision that would let her see past the words to the motivation and intent. But all she had to go on was what she could see and hear with her non-superhero eyes and ears. Franco wanted to have lunch, wanted to be friends, and while she didn't necessarily need another friend, if she were looking, then the Franco she remembered—before their rift—was exactly the kind of person she'd pick for the job. Honorable, kind, smart, and funny. Everything she'd seen so far signaled Franco was still that person. And she was perfectly capable of striking a balance between friendship and professionalism. Her relationship between Wren and Lennox was evidence of that. Besides, if she could assign an appropriate label to whatever this was between her and Franco, she could stop dwelling on the definition and move forward. Friendship was harmless enough, and if she was going to try friendship with Franco, lunch seemed like a harmless way to start.

No pressure. I promise I'll get the earring back to you either way.

She read the words a half dozen times until she could feel Franco worrying she'd overreached. Franco was trying and the least she could do was to try too. It was only lunch, after all.

Unless it wasn't.

Too much thinking. In or out. Her thumbs hovered over her phone, and suddenly she had a brilliant idea. Well, maybe not brilliant, but a way to pretend like this wasn't a date. Not that lunch with an old friend was a date, but Franco was more than an old friend, so…

She typed the words before she could change her mind. *I'll go to lunch with you, but then will you go with me to check something out?*

She started to set her phone down to keep from being hyper-focused on waiting for a reply, but it buzzed in her hand before she could release it from her grasp. The words on the screen made her smile.

Sounds intriguing. I'm in.

Relief stretched its way through her body, quickly followed by a surge of anxiety or excitement—she wasn't sure which. Either way, she was about to see Franco again and she had no regrets.

❖

Franco tilted the basket of chips toward her and plucked another one from the bunch, determined to make it her last.

"It's futile," Nina said.

She raised her eyebrows in a silent question.

"You know that as long as the evil waiter keeps filling that basket, you're going to keep eating those chips." Nina reached for the basket and scooped out a handful. "You may as well stop pretending that one will be your last." She dipped a chip into the tangy salsa. "Some things never change."

Franco relaxed into the comfort of being with someone who knew her so well despite the many years that had passed since they'd spent significant time together. From the moment Nina had picked her up at Pop's house, to this trip to Joe T. Garcia's where they shared their love of fajitas back in the day, this entire day had been a welcome walk down memory lane, and she was finding it easy to pretend nothing had ever come between them. *Live in the moment. It might not last, but enjoy it while it does.*

Easy instructions to follow when Nina was playing the game as well, but Franco was still hesitant about getting comfortable with this new normal when she wasn't sure exactly what the other thing was Nina had planned for them today.

"You're probably wondering why I made you come all the way to Fort Worth for lunch," Nina said.

There she went again. "How do you do that?"

Nina grinned. "Do what?"

"You know exactly what I'm thinking about. I mean you always were good at reading my mind, but that was when we spent every waking moment together."

The grin dimmed slightly. "I have to admit, I spent a lot of time purging you from my memory banks. For months, everywhere I went, I'd think, 'Franco would love that. I wish Franco was here to see this.' It was a big barrier to moving on."

The words were bittersweet, but Franco needed to hear the rest. "But you eventually did."

Nina dipped her hand in the chip basket again and took her time chewing. "In a way, yes. I mean I've had relationships, but none that I would consider serious. I guess my career has been the most meaningful relationship to date, which, now that I've said that out loud, sounds kind of pathetic."

Nina's wistful tone tugged at Franco's heart, but she knew it wasn't her place to say something comforting in response since she was partly to blame for Nina's personal life not turning out the way she'd planned. She stuck with what she thought was the safer side to comment on. "Nothing pathetic about being on the bench. It was a helluva way to find out, but when I realized you'd become a judge, I was really happy for you."

"All part of the grand plan." Nina sighed and pushed the basket away. "But the drawback of being a judge is that you only get to hear about the facts of the case through the lens of everyone else who's worked on it. I miss that part of being a prosecutor—talking to witnesses, making deals with defense counsel, showing up with the cops at a crime scene." She signaled the waiter for the check. "Speaking of which, I pulled the address of the drug house where Daniel Roy supposedly murdered a guy and it's about three miles from here. Want to take a look?"

Franco spotted the spark in Nina's eyes and thanked the universe for its return. "Absolutely."

Nina insisted on paying the bill, a move Franco figured was more about propriety than anything else, and as soon as the waiter returned her credit card, they left the restaurant and headed south. They'd driven for about fifteen minutes, when Franco noticed the frown appear on Nina's face.

"What's wrong?"

Nina pulled over to the side of the road and punched a few buttons on her phone, but the frown only grew deeper. She pointed to the left. "It should be right there."

Franco looked up to see a large, mixed-use development. Loft apartments, restaurants, shopping. The area was crawling with pedestrians, but they all looked more like upwardly mobile locals than junkies looking for their next fix. "How long has it been?"

"He was sentenced four years ago, so a few months longer than that."

"I'm guessing someone decided to clean up the neighborhood."

"I can't believe I didn't check this out before dragging us all the way out here."

Nina's disappointment was palpable, and Franco wanted

nothing more than to make it disappear. "You didn't know. How could you?" She reached over and placed a hand on Nina's. Gently, slowly, so as not to spook her into pulling back, and mentally sighing with relief when she didn't. With her other hand she pointed at a parking space on the next block. "Why don't you pull in there and let's look around. You never know what we might find."

Nina brightened a bit, which told her she'd said exactly the right thing, but when Nina pulled her hand away to get out of the car, Franco instantly missed the connection. This friendship thing was going to be harder than she'd anticipated.

They walked down the block in comfortable silence until they reached the large glass double doors that led to the apartment portion of the building which reminded Franco a lot of the complex where she lived in Houston. When she'd first moved in, it had seemed like the perfect place. Easy access to downtown, loaded with amenities, including a state-of-the-art gym, pristine pool, and a nice variety of restaurants mere steps from her door. She'd taken advantage of every feature for the first month, but as her career took off, recreation took a back seat to success, and she celebrated courtroom wins by taking on more work. It was easy to get caught up in the cycle. Every time she won a big case, her phone lines jammed with calls from defendants seeking the same level of success for their situations. She'd been blessed with business, but there wasn't much time for anything else, and while this trip to Dallas wasn't a vacation, it was the closest thing she'd had to one in as long as she could remember.

"What are you thinking?" Nina asked.

"I don't get to do a lot of this anymore."

"Have lunch with a judge who happens to be your ex-girlfriend?"

Franco laughed. "That for sure." She pointed at the building.

"And also this. You know, go check out a scene. My criminal law professor, Dr. March, held up a pair of worn leather boots the first day of class, and he said, and I'm paraphrasing here, I'm going to make you regurgitate a lot of case law. You'll recite summaries and squirm under my punishing Socratic method. Eventually, we'll get to the stuff that'll matter when you're handling a real case for a real defendant, but in the meantime, if you walk away from this case with only one nugget of useful information, let it be this. Boots on the ground. There is no substitute for seeing something for yourself. It's the bedrock of our trial system. Every juror wants to hear from a witness who saw what happened, but that person may not exist, or they may be completely unreliable. You can be the witness. Go to the scene, listen to the people, see the sights, smell the smells. You may not be able to testify, but if you've done the legwork, you'll be able to weave a narrative the jury will be compelled to believe."

"Wow, that's a powerful message. And absolutely true."

"It was and I used to follow his advice. And then I stopped going. I send associates now, after I've given them some version of March's speech, but I have a feeling March would be disappointed if he knew that now I delegate the work."

"It's never too late to change."

Franco stared hard into Nina's eyes, wondering if she meant that conclusion to apply to all situations or just this one, but she was hesitant to push the point by asking the question out loud. Instead she changed the subject. "Who's handling Daniel's appeal?"

"No one yet. It's a long shot and there aren't a lot of reputable appellate attorneys who will take money when they think there's not much they can do. Lennox and Wren have been combing through the record for any sign of a procedural error, and they have Skye Keaton looking for an evidentiary angle." She pointed to her own chest. "And I suppose I've unofficially appointed myself as the backup lawyer, but the truth is none of us can work on Daniel's case in any official capacity because of the obvious conflicts with our positions."

Franco's brain started churning, but before she could flesh out the thought, she was distracted when a group of people outside of the building walked away, exposing a large sign their presence had hidden from view. *Rodeo Plaza. A Benton Enterprises Development.*

Without thinking, she grabbed Nina's arm and raised it in the direction of the sign. "Do you see that?"

Nina squinted her eyes against the sun. "What?"

"The sign. Benton Enterprises. That's Harry Benton's company, isn't it?"

"Yes." Nina spoke the word casually at first, but then her wide eyes registered the recognition. "Hell of a coincidence, don't you think?"

"Uh-huh." Franco stared at the sign, unable to look away. "What else used to be on this block?"

"I'm not sure. The police report listed a homeless encampment and a convenience store, but not much else. Probably more of the same."

Franco made a mental list of the facts she knew. Daniel Roy had been arrested for a crime committed here and he had no memory of any of his actions the night of the murder. At some point later, the drug house and all the other dilapidated buildings on the street had been torn down and replaced with this bright and shiny beacon to capitalism.

She couldn't help but compare Daniel's situation with Devon's. Both young men who'd suffered a memory loss only to wake to the horror of having serious charges leveled against them.

She looked back at the building. The person who stood to

benefit the most from the demise of what used to stand on this spot was Harry Benton, but he'd also been the one who'd lost the most in Devon's situation—his only daughter, who friends and family say he adored. She was overreaching—trying to find connections where none existed. Boots on the ground weren't there to deliver her to fantasyland.

"Now I really want to know what you're thinking," Nina said. "By the look on your face, I'd think you were watching a movie in slow motion."

Franco figured she'd sound like a crazy person if she shared her real thoughts, so she smiled and shrugged. "Just trying to imagine this place the way it used to be."

"It's hard. Gentrification erases everything in its path." Nina held her hand over her eyes and looked directly into the sunlight. "Is that ice cream over there? With the big waffle cones in the window?"

Franco followed the line of her gaze, grateful for the distraction. "Dipped in chocolate and sprinkles? Why yes, I believe it is."

"I'm going to need some of that stat. And then we'll know this trip was not a waste."

Franco led the way to the ice cream shop, trying to appear patient when all she wanted to do was be in front of her laptop researching the ideas that were percolating faster than she could process. The theory that was forming was crazy, but she couldn't dismiss it out of hand. And she also couldn't talk to Nina about it, which was disappointing but necessary, because if she was right, there was going to be a shitstorm and everyone was going to get caught in it.

CHAPTER EIGHTEEN

Franco walked through the halls of the jail, and this time wasn't as triggering as the time before. Time and distance had been how she'd prevented the recurrence of feelings about her own record, but the trepidation she'd felt the first time she'd gone to see Devon was proof that neither had worked to curb the effect. Pushing through her fears was a much more effective way to put it behind her. For good.

She didn't have to wait long before they brought Devon into one of the visiting rooms. He perked up when he saw her and looked over his shoulder at the guard as if the glance would get him to clear the room faster. When the door finally shut behind him, he was vibrating with excitement.

"You came."

"Of course. Your mom called and said you needed to see me." Franco didn't confess that she'd ducked Jenna's call, letting it go to voice mail. "I was going to come anyway this week. I tried to get in to see you last week, but there was a lockdown every time I came by, and the video equipment at the courthouse wasn't working. Not the stuff for defense lawyers that is. Anyway, I'm glad we have a chance to talk face-to-face. Did you get a copy of my entry of appearance?"

"I did." He pulled at the back of his jumpsuit like it was giving him a wedgie. "What changed your mind?"

"Let's just say I enjoy a good fight." She shoved her notebook to the side and placed both palms down on the small shelf meant to provide her with a writing surface. "What did you want to talk about?"

He fidgeted for a moment before saying, "You go first."

She fixed him with an intense stare, but when he continued to squirm, she decided to comply. "Last time we met, I got the impression you're not a big fan of Lacy's father. Is that because of all this or did you not care for him before?"

Devon's eyes widened in surprise, which was good. She wanted whatever he had to say to be spontaneous because in her experience that made it more likely to be true.

"I always thought he was a good guy. Savvy businessman, big supporter of the fraternity, and he seemed like a loving father."

If he'd dropped the clue any harder, it would've smashed to pieces on the floor. "What changed your mind on that point?"

He shifted in his chair and looked like he was considering busting loose. But he had nowhere to go, and she wasn't leaving until she was satisfied she had all the information she needed to either prove or disprove her theory. "Lacy dropped little hints about his temper," he said. "I saw it in action once when I was at their house."

The next few moments were stuffed with silence—impending doom kind of quiet. Franco wanted to push him to speak, spill whatever it was he was intent on not saying out loud, but she knew filling the space with her own words would only give him cover to keep whatever secret was festering inside. Was he about to confess?

"And he abused her."

After delivering the bombshell, Devon stared at the wall behind her instead of meeting her eyes, and she let the words hang in the air for a moment, certain she already knew who the pronouns belonged to, but not wanting to assume. When Devon continued to stare into space, she gently urged him along. "Lacy's dad abused her?"

"Yes."

"He hit her?"

"No. Not that way."

Franco repressed a gag. The most common form of sexual abuse was familial, but she would never understand how a parent, the person who was supposed to protect their children from harm could be the abuser. "What did she tell you about the abuse?"

"She didn't." He rubbed his temple with his fist like he was trying to jog loose information. "She had a journal. She was supposed to stay with me that night, and I found it in her stuff during the party when I went to get some cash during the party."

"And you read it?" She was careful to keep her voice free from any accusation.

"Parts. Enough. I know it wasn't right, but once I saw what she wrote about him, I couldn't stop. I was devouring it when she caught me."

"And this was during the party."

"Yeah. I'm sorry I didn't tell you before."

"Did you share this information with the police?"

He shook his head. "I only just remembered it this morning. The very first thing I did was call my mom and ask her to let you know I needed to see you."

What were the odds they'd both wanted to discuss Lacy's dad? She decided to take it as a sign instead of a mere coincidence. "What did Lacy say when she caught you reading her journal?"

"She was pissed. She had a right to be, I guess. I shouldn't have gone through her stuff, but I wasn't trying to spy on her. Once I started reading, I couldn't stop."

Franco felt the anticipation building, but she didn't want to rush this story. "What happened next?"

Devon sighed. "I don't know."

"Are you sure about that?" Franco found it hard to believe he'd had a sudden recollection about reading the journal, but then his memory faded out again. "Anything you remember. Anything at all could be important."

"Don't you think I know that?" He fisted his hands and dug them into his thighs. "Some of the guys said they saw us fighting, but I don't remember that. I mean, I know she was mad, but we were in my room when we argued. I don't know if I even went back to the party. She must've left at some point because when I woke up the next morning, she wasn't there, and neither was her stuff."

"Okay." He seemed sincere, so she decided to give this line of questioning a rest for now. "Have you spoken with Lacy's dad since that night?"

"Are you kidding me? I'm the last person he wants to talk to, and I sure don't want to talk to him."

"Your mom told me he funded the scholarship for you to be in the fraternity. I guess I figured you might have a decent relationship with him because of that."

"Yeah, no. Guy just wanted me to be good enough for his daughter. Ironic, right?"

It was ironic, but that didn't make him different from other protective fathers. She needed more. "You said you saw something he did to Lacy when you were at their house that made you suspect all wasn't well between them. What was it?"

"It's kind of hard to describe."

"Try me."

He tugged at his jumpsuit again. "I dunno. He's got this massive study at his house, like a library with bookshelves from the floor to ceiling and a built-in bar with like every kind of liquor you could imagine. He had some of the brothers and a few pledges over for drinks. Lacy came in the room and he made a big deal about how she was his daughter and look how beautiful she is and then he made some comment about the dress she was wearing." He frowned. "It was pretty short."

"Sounds like typical dad-daughter stuff to me."

"Yea, but he kept going on about it. Like Trump going on about Ivanka. It was really uncomfortable."

"I'll agree that's gross, but what made you think it was abusive?"

"She asked to talk to him out of the room. I was near the door, and I heard them talking. She told him she didn't like it when he talked to her like that in front of other people, and he was angry about it. You could hear it in his voice."

What Devon described could be nothing more than an overly doting dad embarrassed to be called out by his daughter in front of his fraternity minions. Or not. She was determined to find out which scenario was true. She pulled out a pen and a piece of paper. "Who else was at the Bentons' house that night?"

She took down the names, one of which she recognized as the pledge Devon had mentioned was running the keg the night of the party when Lacy had gone missing. When she left the jail a few minutes later, she wasn't sure she was any wiser, but she was focused on finding out everything she could about Harry Benton because her gut told her he was the key to this case. Her first instinct was to go to Nina and talk to her about her hunch, but she was the one person off-limits when it came to this case. She'd have to find some other reason to see Nina because after spending the day with her on Saturday, she'd thought of little else since.

CHAPTER NINETEEN

Nina changed outfits three times before settling on a striking emerald green suit with a pale green blouse. Last time she'd worn it, she'd gotten a ton of compliments, and with the election a month away, compliments could translate to votes, and she needed plenty of those if she was going to win reelection. The last few weeks, her opponent, Jerry Donaldson's campaign had surged in the polls, and if his momentum kept going, he would soon be within striking distance from what had been considered a sure win for her. The source of Donaldson's recent success was no secret. His campaign finance reports showed a heavy influx of contributions from conservative PACs, many of which had ties of some kind or another to groups supported by Benton Enterprises, and she was certain the connections were no coincidence.

She buttoned her blouse, put on her suit jacket and jade earrings, and faced the full-length mirror in her bedroom. *Screw you, Harry Benton. I'm not responsible for your daughter's death and I'm not your puppet. And I'm going to kick Jerry Donaldson's ass on Election Day, just you wait.*

Satisfied with her pep talk, she ordered a Lyft and went outside to wait for the car. She wouldn't ever get intoxicated at these campaign events, but she'd have an obligatory drink or two, and election season wasn't the time to have to explain to any police officer that the alcohol they smelled on her breath wasn't her being drunk, it was only her being electable. It was easier to have someone else do the driving.

Tonight's event was for a group of Democratic judges running for reelection, which took the pressure off her to be the main event. She walked into the ballroom at the hotel, took a deep breath, and braced for yet another campaign event. She could do this. She'd make the rounds, give a one-minute speech, clap for her fellow judge candidates, and then she'd be free to find her friends and go to dinner.

The evening was going according to plan. She stepped down from the dais and shook a few hands on her way out of the private room to the main dining area. She scanned the booths, surprised when she didn't spot Lennox and Wren. Maybe they'd gone to the bar to wait. She started to head that way when she felt a tap on her shoulder.

"Judge Aguilar?"

The woman who'd tapped her smiled as Nina turned in her direction. "Your friends asked me to send you to their table when you arrived. Follow me, please."

Nina complied, surprised when the woman walked her back through the dining room she'd just searched, but there was still no sign of her friends. The woman finally stopped in front of a large screen/room divider. "Here they are," she said, motioning to the other side of the screen.

This was different. Nina stepped forward into the space on the other side of the screen and then took a step back when she saw who all was sitting at the table. What was happening?

"Nina, we can see you," Lennox called out. "Come back."

She stood perfectly still for a moment as if the lack of movement would somehow change who was here and what that meant, but as the seconds ticked by it seemed silly to pretend her friends weren't sitting less than six feet from her with Franco smack dab in the middle. If she could work a room of campaign donors, she could deal with this—a mantra she repeated on a loop as she walked into the small private dining area and greeted the group waiting for her there.

"This looks like trouble," she said, noting private investigator Skye Keaton was sitting next to Lennox. Only a few months ago, Lennox would've scoffed at the idea of breaking bread with Skye, who had a colorful past as both a cop and a PI. Add Franco to the mix, and she feared she'd crossed into another dimension. She sat down in the empty seat next to Lennox, directly across from Franco. "What are you all up to?"

"Only good," Franco said. "I promise."

Nina met her eyes and tried to read beyond the words. She'd had a great time in Fort Worth with Franco and had marveled since at how easy it had been to slip back into the comfort of the relationship they used to have. Since then, she'd bottled the feeling, opening it now and then to enjoy the aroma, but then shutting the lid like too much would cause an overdose from which she would not be able to recover. Her caution was born of fear this truce was only temporary. Even if she were to consider trying to recapture what she'd had with Franco, it wouldn't be easy. They lived in different cities, and their careers were likely to come between them. They weren't wide-eyed kids anymore with a future waiting to be dreamed. They were adults with obligations and responsibilities, and the naiveté that she'd once had that caused her to believe their relationship could withstand anything had long since withered away. But as she looked into Franco's eyes, she wanted to believe they could find a way back to each other. Did Franco want that too?

Suddenly, she remembered she and Franco weren't sitting

here alone. "You better share some more details because I'm beginning to think this is a plot to overthrow my campaign."

"Not at all. We were discussing Daniel Roy."

"And you didn't want to include me in the conversation?"

"We were protecting you." Franco paused for a few beats. "Because we were also talking about Devon Grant in the same conversation."

Nina looked around the table, watching all the faces trained on hers, expectant and excited. "I don't get it."

Franco shifted her attention to Lennox. "Maybe you should tell her?"

"Franco thinks Harry Benton is somehow involved in both of these cases."

Lennox dropped the words like a stack of bricks, and Nina appreciated her getting right to the point, but it took her a minute to process what she was hearing. "Wow, okay. And?"

Lennox motioned to Skye. "Franco hired Skye to look into it, and early signs are she agrees there's some kind of connection in both cases to Benton."

"Is there some reason Franco couldn't tell me this herself?" Nina asked, feeling silly about discussing Franco in the third person when she was sitting two feet away.

Lennox flicked a look at Franco and then back to her. "She's trying to protect you. Harry Benton is already funneling tons of money to Donaldson. If he thinks you're involved in any way in us looking into him, then he may not limit his revenge to funding your opponent."

Nina bristled at the implication she would shield her career from harm at the expense of justice, but in her heart she knew that's not what Lennox meant. Her friends were only looking out for her. "Are you about to share with me any information that could affect the outcome of a case pending in my court?"

"Maybe," Lennox said, "but I spoke with Johnny, and as his supervisor, we agreed I could tell you what you need to know in order to accomplish what we have in mind." She gestured to Franco who nodded. "Nothing ex parte here."

Nina's brain told her she should leave and not risk any appearance of impropriety that could jeopardize her campaign, but Lennox had a good point. If attorneys from both sides to a case came to her in chambers, together, and agreed to discuss certain facts of a pending matter, she'd hear them out—no problem. That this discussion was taking place at a restaurant outside of office hours shouldn't make her decision about whether to participate any different. Besides, she trusted these people. Yes, even Franco, because she knew deep down that every decision Franco had made, even the bad ones, was done with good intentions.

"Fine. I'll listen to what you have to say, but if at any point I think we're crossing an ethical line, then I'm out of here. Fair enough?"

"More than fair," Franco said. "I'm going to preface this by saying that I know this sounds a little far-fetched, but the idea came to me when I saw the sign for Benton Enterprises at the development in Fort Worth."

Nina nodded, grateful Franco didn't include the reference to them both making the trip last weekend because she hadn't told anyone else she'd seen Franco outside of the courthouse and Friday night's dinner at Lennox and Wren's. "I'm bracing myself for far-fetched. Bring it on."

"It seemed odd to me that in both cases," Franco said, "the defendant had no memory about a significant portion of their evening. Granted, Daniel Roy had a drug problem, but there were other people who'd been at the drug house that night, before the shooting, that gave statements to the police, and none of them professed not to remember portions of the evening. Same goes for the Sig Ep party Devon was at the night Lacy went missing. Everyone was drinking beer from the same keg, but Devon is the only one who was out cold and has only sketchy memories about portions of the evening."

"Are you telling me you think Harry Benton wanders the city drugging people?" Nina asked with a forced smile. She was only half kidding because this theory was starting out on the way far-fetched side of rational.

Franco glanced around at the others before returning Nina's smile. "I seriously doubt Harry Benton went near the drug house where Daniel was found, but we know for a fact he was at the Sig Ep party at some point during the evening. No, the connection is more about what he had to gain in each situation.

"The area in Fort Worth where Rodeo Plaza now sits was not only the location of the house where Daniel was arrested, but it also was home to several businesses—a couple of convenience stores, a car wash, and a few other mom-and-pop type stores, all of which had received purchase offers from Benton Enterprises in the months before the murder. They all steadfastly refused to sell, even after Benton doubled the offers."

"I guess they knew the value of their property better than he thought," Nina said, still not following Franco's line of thought.

"You're absolutely right. Skye talked to several of them this week, and they said they had a loosely organized merchants association. They'd all agreed to stand strong and hold out for the best offer."

"They must've made a fortune because that place is hopping with business now."

"Hardly. After Daniel was arrested, pled guilty, and was sent to prison, a group of 'concerned citizens' called Save the City started a petition claiming the murder demonstrated the entire area was unsafe and demanding action. The city took up the matter in an expedited session. Days later, the drug house was condemned and the city took the rest of the block in eminent domain. A month later, they voted to give Benton Enterprises a big tax incentive to build Rodeo Plaza on the very same spot."

"I'm guessing Harry Benton has some friends on the Fort Worth city council," Nina said, knowing he probably had friends in local government all over North Texas.

"He does," Wren chimed in. "But not enough to get the deal done through regular channels. I talked to my parents since they run in the same business circles, and they said that Benton has been trying to get the Rodeo Plaza development done for a couple of years. The local business holdouts, along with the fact the area didn't have the infrastructure necessary to support the project, bogged down the process, but Daniel's arrest became a rallying point for the leaders of Save the City, none of whom appear to actually live in that area, based on what Skye found."

"It's true," Skye said. "From what I can tell, Save the City came into being days after Daniel was arrested."

Nina shook her head. "I'm not sure I'm following. Do you all think that this Save the City group is fake?"

"Oh, they are very real," Franco said. "But I don't think they're interested in saving the city so much as making sure that Harry Benton gets to build what he wants and where." She handed a piece of paper to Nina. "Look at the name of the law firm that set up the group's tax-exempt status."

She skimmed the paper, finding the information Franco

referred to at the bottom. She looked at Wren. "Dunley Thornton is your old firm."

"It is. And Gloria Leland still works there."

Nina kept staring at the paper, trying to make sense of the series of coincidences. Gloria Leland was Lennox's old girlfriend and she'd represented Daniel, encouraging him to take a quick and not great plea deal against Lennox's wishes. Gloria had a reputation for not always playing by the rules, but even so, Nina had a hard time believing Gloria had set Daniel up to further the interests of another client. She turned to Lennox. "I thought you were the one who hired Gloria to work on Daniel's case?"

"She volunteered, and of course I accepted. I will never forgive myself for that, but she had a lot of impressive wins on her résumé."

"She sold Daniel out," Franco said. "If the case had gone to trial, it's possible someone would've figured out that instead of a fight over drugs resulting in murder, Daniel himself was drugged. I spoke to my pal in Tarrant County. The police didn't check his hands for gunshot residue because they found the gun in his hand, so there's no way to prove whether he actually fired the gun. He had ketamine in his system, which the prosecutor wrote off to his history of drug use, but nothing in his past indicated that was his drug of choice."

Nina looked around the table at the determined faces of her friends looking back at her. The lawyer part of her wanted to point out the pitfalls of their theory. Daniel might not have normally used ketamine, but a junkie would often make choices according to availability, not preference. Benton Enterprises' desire to put in a mixed-use development in a formerly sketchy neighborhood wasn't by itself a nefarious act. Gloria Leland was a confirmed bitch and she walked a thin line when it came to ethics, but Daniel had to sign off on the plea deal and stand up in open court and admit he killed the victim.

But the judge part of her held her tongue. She could tell by the way the rest of the group was practically vibrating that the Rodeo Plaza development was only part of the story. "Tell me what else you've got."

CHAPTER TWENTY

Franco looked over at Lennox who nodded for her to continue. "I think Harry Benton may have been involved in Lacy's death." She stopped and watched Nina's expression morph from somber consideration to incredulity. "I can explain why."

"Then you better get started, because accusing a father of killing his own daughter is a big deal."

Franco wished they were alone for this conversation. She'd be able to speak more casually, pick up the easy shorthand she and Nina once had that had shown signs of coming back during their outing to Fort Worth. But having Nina's group of friends present helped bolster the argument she was about to make, and ultimately, this was about saving Devon from being convicted for a crime he didn't commit, not winning back a lost love no matter how much she'd prefer the latter.

"I'll confess it's mostly just a hunch right now, but here's what I know. Before the Sig Ep mixer started, Lacy dropped her bag in Devon's room at the house. Devon doesn't remember much about the evening aside from finding a journal in Lacy's things, arguing with her about it, and waking up the next morning to the police knocking on his door."

"And what does any of that have to do with Harry Benton?" Nina asked.

"Devon read portions of Lacy's journal. The entries were about her father." Franco paused before delivering the bombshell, and then deciding it was best to say it as quickly as possible and be done. "Benton was abusing his daughter."

She watched various emotions play out on Nina's face, but Nina didn't say anything. "Did you hear me?"

"I heard you. Do you have any proof?"

"Devon read Lacy's journal, and when he tried to talk to her about it, she went off on him, but she didn't deny what she'd written."

"And I assume you have this journal?"

"No. The police found Lacy's bag in Devon's room, but there was no journal."

"Okay."

Franco recognized the tone in the one word for what it was—dismissal. "Pretend for a minute that you believe Devon. He supposedly got in a fight with Lacy at the party, kills her, dumps her body miles away, comes back to the house, and sacks out in his room with all of her stuff still there until the police show up to arrest him. I mean, I know college freshmen can make dumb mistakes." She waited a few beats to acknowledge she'd engaged in her own share of stupid decisions. "But for a kid with no history of violence, that version of the facts is a stretch."

She motioned to Skye. "There's another possible version, and that's the version we were discussing before you got here." She took the envelope Skye handed her and pulled out the phone camera photos she'd had blown up into eight-by-tens. "I gave Lennox a copy of these."

Nina pulled the photos toward her. "What am I looking at?"

Franco pointed at the man in the right-hand corner of the first one. "That's Harry Benton. He's a little grainy in this enlarged version, but I can show you the original if you want to see for yourself."

"I'm willing to assume it's him for now."

Franco set down two more photos, showing him in different places in the room. "In this last one, which has the latest time stamp, he's standing right next to the entrance to the hall that leads to Devon's room." She pointed at his arm. "See that? It looks like a journal to me."

She watched Nina squint at the photo. It had taken several viewings for her to focus in on the journal, so she didn't expect Nina to see it on the first try.

"It could be a journal but that doesn't necessarily prove it was Lacy's, and even if it was, it doesn't prove what it said. Where did you get these photos?"

"From one of those picture sites," Skye said. "The Greeks all have them—everyone uploads their photos to the site after the party and then people can download what they want or order prints." She grimaced. "You wouldn't believe some of the pictures these kids put out there in the world for anyone to see."

"What are you, one hundred?" Nina teased her. "Social media is crawling with embarrassing photos." She picked up the photo and held it closer to her face. "Lennox, you're here representing the prosecution. What's your opinion about whether there really was a journal and what it might have said?"

Franco held her breath while she waited for Lennox to respond. Her relationship with Lennox had been tenuous from the start, but it seemed they'd found a common cause, at least for now.

"I don't know," Lennox said. "But I'm open to hearing more."

"That's all we want," Franco said. "An opportunity to learn more."

"Are you suggesting I sign a warrant for you to search Harry Benton's house?" Nina asked.

"That would be great, but I doubt you'd agree to that based on what we have so far."

"You'd be right about that." Nina reached for the still full water glass in front of Franco's plate. "May I?"

"Of course." Franco waited while Nina took a long, deep drink and wished they were sitting around a table, having dinner just for fun without the sordid allegations of this case curbing the mood. With Nina all to herself would be ideal, but if it wound up being with this group of friends, she'd love it all the same. Her manic work schedule in Houston meant she had little time to cultivate friendships, and she was beginning to realize how much she missed out on all for the sake of success. Funny how her office had managed to function fine without her since she'd been in Dallas. It called into question all of the focus she'd put on career over personal life, and she suspected she'd always done so because she'd given up on the only person she really ever wanted so very long ago.

"If you don't want a warrant, then what are you asking for?"

Nina's question was directed at the group, but it was a loaded question, nevertheless. Thankfully, Lennox spoke first.

"I spoke with Johnny, and if the defense wishes to renew their motion for a bond reduction, we have no objection, provided there are certain conditions to ensure Mr. Grant appears in court. I'm thinking an ankle monitor."

Nina raised her eyebrows before turning back to Franco. "And I assume you'll be filing that motion right away?"

"Yes, but..." Her next ask was more of a stretch, but she hoped Nina would go for it for her own sake as well as to ensure their plan would work. "I'd respectfully ask that you seal the order and the conditions of the bond."

"Hmmm." Nina steepled her fingers and looked back and forth between her and Lennox. She bit her bottom lip like she always did when she was thinking really hard. "Why do I feel like you two are up to something, and you don't want to tell me because you think I'll say no."

"Don't worry, Judge," Wren said. "If it makes you feel any better, I can vouch for the fact they have a solid plan."

"Solid doesn't necessarily mean good. Besides, I recall not that long ago you were running through the hallway at the courthouse tackling a suspect and busting your Jimmy Choos in the process. Not sure you're the person I trust when it comes to vouching."

"Look," Franco said. "We all understand you're taking a risk by doing this. The election's a month away and when Benton finds out, he's going to come unhinged."

"I'm not scared of Harry Benton."

Nina pushed her plate aside and leaned back in her seat. Franco watched intently, hoping they'd been persuasive enough to convince her to give them a chance to get to the truth, but also feeling a tug of guilt for pushing Nina into doing something that might jeopardize her career. She didn't have to wait long for her response. Nina smacked her palm on the table. "What the hell," she said. "I only ask that you promise me that whatever you have planned, you'll be careful. After the shooting, I'm not interested in anything that puts me or my friends in harm's way. Understood?"

Franco joined the rest of the group, nodding in agreement, both happy and sad to be grouped in with the rest of the friends. Later, when they'd settled the bill and were heading out of the restaurant, she pulled Nina to the side. "Did you drive here or were you planning on having martinis tonight?"

Nina grinned. "I could use a martini after what just happened."

"Let me drive you home." Franco rushed out the words before she lost her nerve.

"Is that your way of inviting yourself for a martini?"

"Is that your way of offering one?" Nina's flirting tone was a good sign. Franco held up her valet ticket. "For real, I'm way better than any rideshare driver. I know exactly where you live, and I have a vested interest in making sure you get home safely."

"Well, when you put it that way."

Franco took her response for a yes and handed the ticket to the valet. Being with the big group had made her feel welcome, but some time alone with Nina, even if only the short drive from the restaurant to her house, was all she really wanted.

❖

Nina pretended to check her email while Franco drove, but her real focus was on the flirtatious banter they'd engaged in at the valet stand. She wasn't sure what she'd been thinking or if she'd been thinking at all. After all her talk about being an impartial jurist, she'd held a mini bond hearing off the record in the middle of a restaurant and now she was being chauffeured home by one of the attorneys in the case.

But Franco wasn't simply a lawyer who happened to be appearing in her court. Franco was the one who walked away. The one she hadn't been able to forget. And now she was back in her life, personal and professional, and her focus was fractured precisely when it needed not to be. She thought back to what Keene had told her when she tried to get the case transferred to another judge. *You're uniquely qualified to compartmentalize your feelings in favor of the facts.* Yes, that had been the case, once upon a time, but now…Now, she wasn't so sure.

"Any important emails?"

She looked up from her phone without a clue as to what was on the screen. "No. Just random stuff."

"Are you okay? You seem distracted."

Distracted. That was a good word for it. "That was a lot to take in back there."

"Do you want me to tell you what we have planned?"

She barely considered the offer before rejecting it. "I think we've blurred enough lines lately. You do you, and I'll hear about it when it's done."

Franco pulled into her driveway and turned off the engine. "May I walk you to the door?"

"Sure." Nina shrugged like it didn't matter to her either way. But it did, and when Franco hesitated, she reached for Franco's hand and squeezed. "Please."

It didn't take long for them to reach the door. Nina counted each of the twenty-one steps, and when they reached the porch, she instantly regretted wasting the short journey focused on its end. She pulled out her key and shoved it into the lock. Before she could turn the key, Franco's hand closed over hers, and the heat of her touch burned through any lingering resolve to ignore the pull of their attraction.

"Inside," she murmured, pushing open the door and tugging Franco along behind her. She kicked the door shut with her heel, unwilling to release her hold. It had been so long since anyone had stirred her to this heady state of arousal. Nineteen years long. She leaned in, eager to recapture the feelings that had eluded her in every other relationship since Franco. How was it possible these feelings were even stronger now?

Stop thinking. Thinking had kept her single all these years. Thinking was what she did every time she compared a date to Franco. Thinking had doomed any chance for more with women who'd made it past the dating phase once she started thinking about the better life she would've had if her one true love hadn't walked away from their dreams. No other woman could live up to the hype in her head.

"What are you thinking?" Franco asked, her voice low and husky with desire.

"Thinking is overrated." Nina put force behind the words. She placed a hand on the side of Franco's face and leaned in. The moment her lips touched Franco's she was home. Warm, comfortable, familiar home. She relaxed into the ease of the kiss, following Franco's lead as if they'd never stopped this dance.

And then Franco dipped her tongue into her mouth, and warm and comfortable turned into a fiery, hot science experiment on the verge of exploding. For all the chemistry they'd had in their youth, she didn't remember anything like the thunderous connection happening right now. She ran her hands along Franco's sides, pulling her closer as their kiss grew deeper. She couldn't think, she couldn't breathe, she was lost and she was exactly where she needed to be. When Franco gently pulled away, she took a deep breath, unsure whether they'd been kissing for hours or only seconds.

Franco leaned her forehead against hers. "That was amazing," she murmured.

"It was."

"You know," Franco said. "I make a really mean martini, if you're still in the mood."

Was it just her or was everything Franco said loaded with innuendo? And she kind of loved it. She started to say yes to the martini when an insistent buzz snapped her out of her trance.

"I think that's your phone," Franco said, pointing at her jacket.

"Sorry." Nina grabbed the offending piece of technology intending to silence it immediately, but when she spotted the text from Detective Beck Ramsey, the spell abated.

"What is it?" Franco asked, her brow furrowed with concern.

"DPD detective needs a warrant." Nina started typing into her phone. "She's coming by now."

"Does she have to?"

Franco leaned in and whispered the words into her ear in a way that made them sound like an invitation rather than a question about her job, and in that moment, Nina wanted to say yes to whatever Franco had to offer, no matter how disconcerting it was to think about the ease with which she was willing to slip back into trusting their attraction. But when the phone buzzed again, it broke the spell entirely.

She stepped out of Franco's embrace, trying desperately to ignore the instant and unwelcome temperature drop by checking her phone again. "She'll be here in fifteen minutes."

"And you want me to be gone when she gets here."

No, that's not what I want, but I don't know if I can handle more kissing with you right now. There wasn't any sense saying the words out loud since they sounded like a future promise—one she wasn't sure she would be able to keep, so she settled on the easier, professional conflict excuse. "Sharing dinner with a group of friends is one thing, but you here at my house with just you and me?"

"It'll look bad." Franco shrugged. "I get it." She walked the short distance to the door but paused with her hand on the knob. "Nina?"

"Yes?"

"I get it, but I don't like it."

Me neither. Nina bit back the words and settled on what she hoped was a perfectly neutral expression meant to convey this was an interesting evening and ending it with a soul-searing kiss from you was the highlight of my life, but you totally get why we have to stay professional, right? Oddly enough, the understanding she saw reflected in Franco's eyes right before she walked out the door signaled her message had been received, loud and clear. Now all she had to worry about was how to keep from kissing Franco again because she was sure that was all she would be thinking about for the foreseeable future.

CHAPTER TWENTY-ONE

H ow do you know the mom again?"
Franco looked up to see Skye staring at her. It was the second time that morning that she'd zoned out while Skye was talking. Her lack of focus had nothing to do with Skye and everything to do with the memory of Nina's lips on hers. Soft, velvet, scotch-kissed lips hungrily devouring her own before she'd stopped abruptly and pulled away.

Franco barely remembered the ride home from Nina's the night before. Pop had been asleep when she got home, and for once she missed his habit of regaling her about whatever he'd watched on TV while she was out. She'd tried to sleep, but the memory of the kiss kept her up late into the night. Teenage Nina had been a great kisser, but Judge Nina Aguilar kissed like a boss, and all Franco wanted was to be lost in her embrace. The abrupt way their evening had ended had left her spending all night wanting more.

But instead of seeing Nina again, she was here at the jail with Skye, waiting for Jenna to show up so they could explain what was going to happen next on Devon's case. She hadn't seen Jenna since the last setting on Devon's case, and she'd purposely avoided Jenna's attempts to reach out to her. Seeing her today, the day after she'd kissed Nina into next week, would be an unwelcome reminder of Jenna's contribution to why she and Nina had missed out on a lifetime together, and on the heels of last night's kiss, the loss felt especially big.

"We went to the same college."

Jenna appeared just then saving her from further questions and blowing into the lobby of the jail like a whirlwind, frantically looking around until she spotted them waiting for her. She rushed over.

"Sorry, I'm late. Traffic. I met with the bondsman like you said. Are they really letting him out?"

Franco held up a hand to stop the stream of questions, annoyed that Jenna was late. Again. "Yes, they are going to let him out, but with conditions." She pointed to a spot on the other side of the lobby, away from the rest of the people entering and exiting the building. When they were huddled in the corner, she noticed Jenna had dark circles under her eyes and her expression was anxious. She was scared for her son and hopeful about his release. The flood of admissions Jenna had made earlier about what had happened after Nina had rejected her came back, and Franco decided Jenna had been punished enough. She might not be able to forget what she'd done, but after all these years, forgiveness was a gift she could give herself.

She set aside her annoyance and took a gentle tone. "He's going to have to wear an ankle monitor. And, as part of the agreement with the prosecutor, he'll be going back to the fraternity house to help with the investigation."

"I don't get it. He has to help the DA make the case against him?"

Franco shot Skye a pleading look and she got the message like a champ. "No. We're doing our best to convince the DA that Devon wasn't involved in Lacy's death, but we need to develop some evidence to support that contention. I could go talk to Devon's fraternity brothers, but they'd be less likely to open up to me than if he has casual conversations with them and reports back."

"What's your theory?"

"We can't tell you," Franco jumped in before Skye could answer, fearing Jenna might go off on her own, trying to gather evidence if she knew what they were after. The last thing she needed was for Jenna to get in the middle of the deal they'd worked out and blow it all to pieces. "Because it could compromise the investigation. You don't want that, do you?"

"Of course not," Jenna replied, puffed up with indignation.

"Great. Then please don't ask Devon about it because it'll be hard for him to have to tell you no."

Jenna ran a finger along her lips and tossed the imaginary key into the air. Franco waited while Skye walked her over to the bond desk, where she signed the necessary paperwork to finish posting bail. Lennox had pulled some strings and, rather than the usual several-hour wait, Devon was released in less than thirty minutes, already fitted with an ankle monitor. Franco let him have a few minutes for an emotional reunion with his mom before she and Skye whisked him out of the jail and down the street to the least popular diner near the courthouse to keep from running into anyone who might overhear their conversation.

Franco waited until Devon had devoured a second helping of chicken fried steak before reviewing the details of their plan. "You understand what you're supposed to do?"

"Sure. You're going to hook me up with a wire and I need to talk to the guys about that night and see if anyone saw Lacy's dad do anything suspicious the night of the party."

"Okay, but maybe don't use the word 'suspicious,'" Franco said. "You're going to have to be subtle. Harry Benton contributes a lot of money to the fraternity. People are going to be hesitant about saying anything bad about him, so your job is to get them to tell you what they saw without passing judgment. Pitch it like you're trying to fill in the pieces of the evening. So, instead of saying something like 'Did you see Harry Benton break into my room and leave with a journal?' go with 'I know I saw Harry walking around in the residence, do you know what time that was?' You may have to drill down a bit, but just be careful not to spook anyone."

"Do you really think he could've killed her?"

Franco wanted to point out that he was the one who first mentioned Harry might be involved, but she could understand why he'd second-guess his own conclusions. "Are you having second thoughts?"

He shook his head vigorously. "Not even. You should've seen her face when I told her I'd read her journal. She totally freaked out. Not like I violated her privacy, but like she was scared for anyone to know about it. I may not remember much else about that night, but I'll never forget the fear in her eyes. It's my last memory of her. If I hadn't passed out, maybe she'd still be alive."

"Have you considered you might have been drugged that night? Someone could've slipped something into your drink."

To her surprise, he seemed unfazed by the suggestion. "I guess so," he said. "I've heard of them doing that to pledges. I guess I thought I'd know if it happened."

If he weren't charged with a first-degree felony, his naiveté might be cute. "There's no way to prove it. The cops didn't order a tox screen when you were arrested, and it would be long out of your system by now. Don't get too deep into it, but if you see an opening, mention how you felt the morning after and see what they say."

"Anything else?"

"No, that's it. Skye has some clothes your mom brought

and she's going to take you somewhere where you can change, and then she'll get you back to campus."

"What about the wire?"

Franco smiled. "You're already wearing it. The microphone is in your ankle monitor. Don't get showy with the monitor, but if someone happens to see it, they'll likely assume it's a condition of bail."

He gave her a thumbs up. "Got it. Keep the monitor on the down low unless absolutely necessary."

She stayed behind for a few minutes after he left with Skye. From her seat in the booth, she could see the courthouse in the distance, and she wondered what Nina was doing at this very moment, and whether Nina had spent as much time thinking about last night's kiss as she had.

She hoped so.

❖

"Guess who's back?"

Nina looked up from her desk at the sound of Reggie's voice to see her standing in the doorway to her temporary office. She wasn't big on guessing, but she knew who she wanted it to be. "Surprise me."

Reggie disappeared and a moment later, Franco entered the room looking fabulous in a charcoal gray suit that showed off her trim, athletic figure. She dropped into one of the chairs and leaned back like she hung out there all the time.

"Either you came to Dallas with a trunk full of clothes or you've been shopping."

Franco grinned. "Or both."

"Unless you've changed a lot, you never were big on shopping."

"True. But I discovered the magic of tailor-made clothes.

You go in once, they take your measurements, and then clothes magically appear on your doorstep." She patted her stomach. "I just have to make sure I stay the same size, which has become a bit of a challenge with Pop's cooking. The man thinks French fries are a vegetable."

Nina dropped her jaw. "They're not?"

"It's a travesty."

They both shared a laugh, and then Franco glanced back at the door. "Mind if I shut that?"

Nina didn't want to deny the request, but her gut clenched as she considered what would happen if someone other than one of her friends found her behind closed doors with the defense attorney on a high-profile case. "Probably best to leave it open." She tried not to wince as she delivered the words, but she immediately felt tension cool the space between them.

"Sure, yeah, okay."

For the first time since she'd wandered back into her life, Franco seemed flustered, and Nina's first instinct was to put her at ease, tell her she could go ahead and shut the door, but she shoved the inclination aside. At some point, Franco was going to go back to Houston, and she'd be here, on her own, back to filling every moment of her life with work to avoid worrying about being the third wheel to her coupled-up friends. It had been nice to reconnect with Franco and clear the air, but to pretend they could pick up where they left off or simply start over was to defy the reality of their situation. Best to get ahead of whatever Franco had come to say. With a cautious glance at the door, she plunged in. "It's been great to spend time with you, but what happened last night can't happen again."

"This case won't last forever." Franco crossed and uncrossed her legs. "And I hear Judge Larabee is on the mend and should be back soon."

"It's not just the case."

"You haven't forgiven me."

"There's nothing left to forgive." Nina waved a hand. "We were kids then. Both of us would probably do things differently now. But that's the point. We're adults. We have different, separate lives."

"I live in Houston and you live in Dallas."

"That's a big part of it, sure."

"What else?"

She should've planned for this conversation, had swift answers prepared, but in the moment, she defaulted back to "we lead different lives."

Franco scooted to the edge of her seat. "Details. We can work through details as long as we agree on the concept."

"We don't." Nina dropped her head. "I don't."

"Nina." Franco's voice was laced with pain. "You don't mean that."

Did she? With Franco sitting right in front of her it was difficult to separate what she wanted from what was best. Was it possible the two could be the same? And what if she gave Franco another chance? What would happen when it was time for her to go home? She wasn't interested in a long-distance relationship. She had a life here and she wanted a partner who could permanently be a part of it, but asking Franco if she'd move back to Dallas seemed premature when they'd only just reconnected. No, with the pending case and the upcoming election and the uncertainty about where Franco would wind up, it was easier to accept the friendship and shelve the rest. "I do, but I want to stay in touch. Be friends."

"Friends." Franco spoke the word like it was a curse. She stood. "From what I've seen you have plenty of friends. They're a good group, but I don't want to be one of the bunch."

She flicked a glance at the open door. "I want something more. If you decide you do too, let me know." She walked to the door. "I won't bother you again."

Nina watched her disappear down the hall, barely resisting the urge to call out after her, chase her down, and tell her she'd changed her mind. Right. She could see the news story now. Judge Aguilar runs through courthouse, chasing defense attorney and professing her undying love.

Wow. Where had that come from? Sure, she'd once loved Franco, but she'd convinced herself those feelings had faded as the years had passed, yet she couldn't deny those old feelings had come surging back the moment she'd spotted Franco standing across from her in the courtroom, just as the shooting started. At the time, she'd thought seeing Franco was somehow prophetic, but only as a sign to live life without regrets because it could be robbed from you in an instant. Could Franco's reappearance in her life mean more than that? Was she foolishly turning down a second chance at love?

She put her head on the desk and surrendered to the feeling of helplessness that enveloped her. She didn't know the answers to these questions, but she did know one thing for sure. Their relationship might not have been permanent, but Franco Rossi had left an indelible mark on her heart.

Chapter Twenty-Two

Franco pulled into the driveway of her dad's house and was just about to open the car door when her phone rang through the speakers, announcing a call from Skye. She pressed the button to connect the call, but didn't get a word in before Skye announced, "Jackpot."

She'd been driving around for the last hour, trying to figure out some way to set aside her feelings for Nina and move on with her life, and she'd been completely unsuccessful. The prospect of a break involving Devon's case was a beacon of hope, and she held on tight. "Tell me."

"That pledge who was working the keg the night of the party, Arnie Landeau? He told Devon he saw Harry Benton coming out of his room that night and he was carrying a book. Benton even held it up and said, 'I'm keeping track of all of you pledges. Make sure you do us proud.'"

The guy had nerve. She'd give him that. "Does he have any idea what time that was?"

"He didn't remember the time, but he said it was within thirty minutes of the second keg being delivered. I called the distributor they purchased the keg from and checked the time. The delivery was at nine fifteen."

"Well after when Lacy left the party."

"Right. And it gets better."

"Don't hold back."

"Arnie saw Lacy earlier in the evening. She walked her dad back to a corner and had an animated conversation. Arnie said she looked angry, but he couldn't make out anything they had to say, and he doubts anyone else heard because the DJ was pretty loud."

"Did he happen to see Devon during any of this?"

"Devon told him he didn't remember much about the party and Arnie said they probably didn't remember because he headed upstairs pretty early. He made some remark about how none of the men in Lacy's life were getting along with her that night."

"Interesting. So, our theory is that after Devon confronted Lacy, she in turn confronted her dad. He lifted the journal from Devon's room, read all of things Lacy wrote about him, either killed her or arranged it, and set Devon up to take the fall, starting with some spiked drinks to make the job easier."

"That's about it. And one more thing. Arnie said that while he was stuck on keg duty most of the night, legacies would relieve him for a few minutes on the hour. Guess who stepped up to do his fifteen minutes right after Lacy left?"

"Harry Benton appears to be a man of many talents," Franco said, trying to summon enthusiasm for Skye's findings. This was great news for Devon as it appeared to corroborate his version of events, but all it meant for her was a trip back to the courthouse to convince Johnny Rigley he had the wrong guy and that he should get a warrant from none other than Nina.

Nope. She couldn't risk seeing Nina again so soon after her overture at something more had been soundly rejected. "Hey, I just pulled up to my dad's place and I've got to help him out with a few things. If I let Johnny know you're on the way, do you mind taking the recording to him? That, along with Devon's statements, should be enough for him to request a warrant to search Benton's house. Let him know that Devon says she had a room there, which means there might be other journals, although by now I'd expect Benton would've rooted out any evidence Lacy had hidden away."

"No problem. I'll text you when I know where things stand."

Franco thanked her and clicked off the call. Normally, she'd want to be in the thick of the investigation, celebrating when she'd scored a victory, but all she felt right now was sad. Seeing Nina again had been the best and worst part of coming to Dallas. If what she believed about Harry Benton was true, then Devon would soon be a completely free man, sans ankle bracelet and all. She on the other hand was chained to the mistakes she'd made in the past. Nina may have loved her once, but too much hurt and too much time had passed for them to make a full recovery, and she'd had no business thinking otherwise.

According to Dr. Mason, Pop's meds were close to being back in balance and he was almost back to his old self. His next doctor visit wasn't until a month from now, and even if Devon wasn't exonerated right away, she could fly back for in-and-out court appearances until the case was resolved. She'd miss spending more time with Nina's friends, but they were Nina's friends not hers, and if she didn't have the Nina part of the equation, she wasn't going to be seeing much of them anyway.

She looked down at her suit. She'd ordered it a week ago and it had been delivered this morning along with three others in anticipation of staying a while, but now they were just more crap she'd have to haul back home. Her empty, lonely home. She turned her attention to her dad's house. The exterior looked ten times better than it had when she'd arrived, and she'd taken pride in doing the work necessary to get it back in shape, but like Nina's friends, this house wasn't hers either. She hadn't realized how empty her life was until she'd arrived back in Dallas and started to populate it with people and places both new and old. For a second, she considered moving back. It would be a hassle to transfer her business, start building a client base here. If Nina had given her a spark of hope, she'd do it in a heartbeat, but she hadn't. If she moved back to Dallas now, she'd spend the rest of her days walking through minefields full of Nina memories and real-life sightings that left her wanting. Better to go back to Houston and file this trip away as closure rather than a new beginning.

But if it was truly better, then why did the prospect of leaving feel so bad?

❖

Nina heard her cell phone ringing, but she couldn't find it, which was crazy since she'd only been home for a half hour or so, barely enough time to pour a martini, let alone lose her phone. Unable to stand the incessant ringing, she tore through the couch cushions and found the noisemaker just in time for the caller to hang up. She started to set it down again, but she spotted words forming on the screen.

Sending officer with affidavit for warrant. Don't go anywhere.

Lennox was too freaking bossy for her own good. The worst part of being a judge was having law enforcement officers show up at her house at all hours expecting her to read and digest arrest warrant affidavits and render legal decisions, when all she wanted to do when she got home was change into comfy clothes and pour a stiff drink. She typed a quick reply: *Better get here fast. I'm ready for joggers and a dirty martini. He'll be quick. Thirty minutes. Tops.*

Not as quick as she'd like, but she took the opportunity to tidy the living room, starting with replacing the couch cushions she just tossed to the floor and arranging the accent pillows. She stood back to admire her work, and the doorbell rang, startling her out of her interior design moment, and she walked to the door and flung it open.

"That was fast," she said, only to immediately cover her mouth with her hand. The guy standing in front of her wasn't an officer of the law. It was Harry Benton, who looked even more like a linebacker when she wasn't standing behind her desk. He pushed the door open farther and stepped into the foyer.

"You were expecting me?" he asked with a smirk.

Nina took a step back and pointed at the phone in her hand. "The police are on their way. You should go."

His laugh was mirthless. "Would you like to guess the identity of the biggest donor for the fraternal order of police? He air-jabbed his finger in her direction. "Go on, guess." When she stayed silent, he got increasingly agitated. "Don't be a spoilsport. Guess."

She'd been around plenty of crazy people in her career, but most of them had been in the courtroom where she'd been surrounded by sheriff's deputies who she assumed would protect her. Of course, after the shooting, she knew that was a fallacy. The good guys with guns would hold their fire rather than risk shooting into a crowd of innocent people to try to take down one shooter. But it would take a lot of nerve for Harry Benton to try to harm her right here in the middle of her living room, so she decided to see what happened when she stood up to the bully.

"Maybe I wasn't clear when I said you should go. I meant leave. Now." She added her own air jab to emphasize the point, while keeping her other hand, the one with the phone in it, behind her back.

"So, I get this call from a buddy of mine," Benton said, not coming any closer, but not leaving either. "He does a lot of off-duty security work for one of my properties. Anyway, he tells me that he got a call to bring a warrant out here for you to sign and my name happens to be on it. Can you believe that?"

"It'll be pretty easy to figure out which officer that was," Nina said, wishing for one of the old push button flip phones from her youth because it would be a whole lot easier to sneak a 911 call on one of those. She frantically pushed buttons on her phone, hoping something would connect, and she talked louder to cover her actions. "It's not like the warrant is going to disappear. If you don't have anything to hide, you shouldn't have a problem with the police doing a routine search."

He stepped closer. "Except there's nothing routine about it. Maybe you don't know this about me, but I'll be perfectly clear. No one messes with my family business. Not a punk kid who thinks he's good enough to date my daughter, and not a liberal judge who thinks she's smarter than I am."

At this point, Nina had given up on blindly touching her phone screen. For all she knew enough time had passed that the screen was locked. She needed a weapon or a fast exit. She faked a glance to the dining room on her left and when he followed her gaze, she whipped her head to the right and the double doors that led to the patio, which unfortunately had a double lock as well. There was no way she could outrun him to the door and get it open in time to escape. Time to shift into stand her ground mode. She had a gun, but it was upstairs in her nightstand. She scanned the room and settled on the Nambé vase on the table in the entry, certain it would pack a decent punch. She was just about to start a sprint in that direction when she caught a glimpse of a car that looked a lot like Franco's pulling up outside on the street.

She shouted at Harry on the off chance her voice might carry or at least cover the sound of anyone approaching to save her ass. And then she prayed she could duck death a second time this month.

❖

Franco wasn't sure what compelled her to drive by Nina's on her way out of town. She told herself the gesture was one final step toward closure, but the closer she got, the more she craved a future with Nina, so she spent the drive practicing her very best pitch for why they should give their love a chance.

She'd settled on the perfect words seconds before reaching Nina's driveway only to find a Bentley parked behind Nina's car. Okay, so Nina had company. Rich company. Franco sat behind the wheel and contemplated her next move. The Bentley was a sign. She should keep driving and stay the course on her original plan. Nina had a full life and there wasn't room for her in it even if Nina wanted to explore something more.

You walked away without giving us a chance.

Nina's words from the past echoed loud. She was doing it again. Choosing the path that took her away from Nina because she had decided it was best for both of them.

No, this time it was Nina who'd decided there was no place for her in her life. But who could blame her? How could Nina trust her to stick around and make things work when she had only ever done the opposite? And here she was, with her packed car, taking off again. If she really wanted a future with Nina, she needed to march right up to her door and tell her she was going to stick around until she convinced her she wanted it too. She shot another look at the Bentley and was assessing her options when she heard a shout that sounded like it was coming from inside the house. Probably nothing, but it was as good a reason as any to knock on the door. She parked her car on the street and started to walk to the door.

As she passed the Bentley, a familiar logo on the bumper caught her eye. It looked like a parking sticker with a picture of a lasso and the words Rodeo Plaza—the development Harry Benton had built on the land in Tarrant County where Lennox's brother had allegedly shot another man in cold blood. Her own blood ran cold, and she ducked behind the car, took a picture with her phone, and texted it to Lennox. *At Nina's. 911.*

The smart thing to do would be to wait for help, but someone in the house was shouting, and there was no good reason for Harry Benton to show up on Nina's doorstep in the evening or ever, for that matter. She ran back to her car and grabbed the lug wrench out of the trunk. She was going in and she wasn't coming out until she was sure Nina was safe.

❖

Nina sat on the couch while Harry loomed over her. She didn't care if they ever turned up evidence to prove it—based on the way he was acting, she had no doubt he'd been involved in his daughter's death. He'd questioned her over and over about the warrant and she insisted she didn't know anything because she hadn't seen the affidavit yet, but she wasn't sure how long she could hold him and his rising temper off.

She'd about given up hope when she spotted a figure moving on the patio. She quickly looked in the other direction, not wanting to give Harry any reason to turn around and see for himself what was going on.

"Last chance," he said. "Tell me what I want to know and I'll consider making a big donation to your campaign."

"What about Donaldson?" she asked, tired of placating this man and deciding to try a different approach. "I doubt he'll do your bidding if you decide to spread the love."

He laughed. "Guess you have some fire in you after all."

His comment sparked an idea. She'd seen no evidence he was carrying a weapon, although he probably didn't need one because he could crush her with his big beefy hands. What she needed was a distraction, something to give her time to get to an escape or give cover to whoever was outside, assuming they were here to help her and not Harry. She didn't have time to think it through. She had to act. She leapt to her feet and started shouting "Fire! Fire!"

His head whipped around and she took off toward the patio doors. She was reaching for the first lock, but her fingers fumbled at the sound of his heavy footfalls coming up behind her. At that second, Franco appeared on the other side of the glass and she waved her to the side. Nina moved out of the way just in time to avoid shattered glass showering the floor. Before she could fully register what was happening, she heard shouts from the front of the house, and the front door crashed inward.

Franco pulled her into her arms and held her tight while uniformed men in tactical gear swarmed her living room, tossing Harry Benton to the floor. She sagged against Franco and sobbed with relief. This house might be where she lived, but in Franco's arms she was finally home.

CHAPTER TWENTY-THREE

"W" ho wants more chili?"

Franco smiled as the entire group packed into Pop's living room turned toward him and waved. He was wearing the Chili Master apron Nina had bought for him when they were in high school, and he was completely in his element cooking for a crowd. Lennox, Wren, Skye, and her wife, Aimee, had all joined her and Nina for an informal debrief after Harry Benton had been processed into the county jail where he was being held without bond.

"Are you sure you're up for this?" Franco whispered to Nina who was tucked up against her on the couch.

"I don't think I'll sleep tonight unless I hear the rest of the story."

She squeezed Nina's hand and held tight while Lennox told her part.

"The officer who was on the way to you with the warrant does indeed do security work for Benton Enterprises, and when he saw Benton's name on the warrant, he called him and gave him a heads-up," Lennox said. "A normal person would call his attorney or go home and hide whatever it was he didn't want the cops to find, but this guy is far from normal and used to getting his way with force. Apparently, he jumped into his one-of-a-kind Bentley and headed out on a mission to threaten a district judge, a mistake he'll do plenty of extra time for."

"Have they found anything at his house yet?"

Lennox consulted her phone—Johnny was at the scene, and he'd been sending text updates. "So far no journal, but they did find a massive walk-in gun safe."

"Of course they did," Nina said.

Lennox held up a finger. "Wait for it." She scrolled on her phone for a moment and then held up a photo. "See this? These are empty shelves. Custom shelves designed specifically to fit whatever guns are to be stored in them."

"Spit it out, dear," Wren said.

"Johnny says at least three of these empty shelves fit the same weapons that were used by the shooter in Nina's courtroom last month. The sheriff's department is seizing all of the ammo they find so they can compare it to the casings from the shooting."

"Do you think it's possible he hired someone to try to kill Devon?" Franco asked, not sure she believed it herself.

"I think with this guy anything is possible," Lennox said. "It's going to take a while to sort out the extent of his involvement in any of these cases, but he's not going anywhere until that happens. If he was as smart as he thinks he is, he would've packed his shit and gotten out of town instead of showing up at Nina's tonight. Thank God you showed up there when you did."

Franco had already told Nina she'd been headed back to Houston, but she couldn't leave without trying one more time to convince her they could make a relationship work. That story was just for them, but to appease the others, she glossed over that part and gave them the rest. "I had to do a double take when I drove up to the house and saw the Bentley in the drive. When I recognized the parking sticker, I suspected something was wrong, but then I heard shouting coming from the house and I knew for sure."

"My loud judge voice was my only weapon," Nina said. "I wasn't convinced anyone would be able to hear me. I felt so stupid letting him in the house, but he took me completely by surprise."

Franco put an arm around her shoulders and pulled her close. "You were amazing. I don't know how you managed to keep him at bay as long as you did."

"Yeah, well, what Lennox said is spot-on. Thank goodness you showed up when you did."

They were both staring into each other's eyes when someone cleared their throat. Franco turned to face the group. "What?"

"You two are a thing?" Skye asked, earning a shove from her wife. "Hey, I didn't know," she said, rubbing her side.

"If it makes you feel better, Skye, I didn't know for sure either until today." Franco felt Nina shift in her arms, and she looked down to see Nina looking up at her. "We're a thing, right?"

Nina's smile was warm and wide and wonderful. "You better believe we are."

Turn the page for a bonus short story

by Carsen Taite from the BSB anthology

Amor and More: Love Ever After

AUTHOR'S NOTE

Skye Keaton was never supposed to be a star. Her very first appearance was in my second novel, *It Should Be a Crime*, and I created her as a foil to the ever-honorable cop turned law student Parker Casey. Skye was dark and dangerous—a seemingly unredeemable bad girl, and her every action allowed Parker to shine in contrast. And while readers unanimously loved Parker, I could never get Skye out of my head because some people are complicated, and those complications make a character interesting. I was intrigued by her unwritten backstory, and in novel number five, *The Best Defense*, I decided to tell Skye's full story, and she's managed to work her way into many of my romantic suspense novels ever since. This story takes place soon after *The Best Defense*, but you'll see her appear again and again in many of my stories since. Let me know if you figure out exactly how many times Skye takes the stage ☺

BORN TO RIDE

If you polish that chrome any harder, you'll put a hole in it."
Skye looked up from her Harley and squinted into the sun. Her best friend, Parker Casey, stood in her driveway, dressed in a sleek suit. A total contrast to her own cargo shorts, tank top, and sweat. She looked down at the torn T-shirt rag in her hand and compared it to the fancy leather briefcase Parker held. They'd first met as fellow cops. Now she was a P.I. and Parker was a lawyer. They still worked on cases together, but she rarely saw Parker in lawyer drag outside of the office. She must've come straight from the courthouse.

Skye's stomach twisted in panic, and she deflected whatever business Parker had come to discuss by pitching the rag at her. "I could use some help. Take the rear fender and make sure you can see the evil in your eyes when you're done."

Parker shook her head but set her briefcase down, rolled up her sleeves, picked up the rag, and elbowed in. "You plan on riding in a parade or something?"

Skye grabbed another rag and went back to work. "Nope. I'm selling her. Got a guy coming by this afternoon to take a look."

Parker stopped rubbing. "No way. You've had this bike as long as I've known you. Does your wife know you're getting rid of your favorite possession?"

"It's not my favorite possession."

"Liar."

"Shut up, Casey. If you don't want to help, get lost." The banter was playful, but Skye meant what she said. She didn't want to talk about it.

Parker threw the worn rag back at Skye. "Well, now that you mention it, I didn't come over to polish the chrome on your ride. We have a hearing scheduled for Thursday. I came by to go over the paperwork. Aimee's office said she was working from home this morning."

Skye's stomach rolled and she struggled to keep the panic from her voice. "Thursday? Next week?"

Another voice interrupted Parker's answer. "What are you two up to?"

Skye tamped down her anxiety and turned to face her wife. Aimee, like Parker, wore a suit, but they couldn't have looked more different. Instead of navy wool with hard lines, hers was bright red and showed off sexy curves. Normally, the sight of her wife all dressed up was arousing, but today it only fueled her sense of foreboding. "Hey, babe, did you know attorneys make house calls?"

"Ours does, anyway." Aimee gave Parker a big hug. "Parker, why don't you come inside where my wife will fix you a drink instead of making you baby her favorite possession." Aimee led them into the house. The moment her back was turned, Parker mouthed "see" and Skye responded by punching her in the arm. The two continued their silent but physical argument until they reached the dining room. When Aimee turned back to them, they froze like two five-year-olds caught in the act.

Aimee cast them a wary look before addressing Parker. "I assume you have the paperwork with you? Why don't you set up in here, and we'll be right back."

Skye watched Parker open her briefcase and line the table with several stacks and rows of paperwork before she followed Aimee to the kitchen. As soon as she crossed the threshold, Aimee swept her into a tight embrace. Skye looked over her shoulder and started to push away, but Aimee murmured, "She's not coming in here. Let me hold you for a minute."

Skye stopped resisting and allowed the warmth of Aimee's closeness to flood through her. The soft waves of Aimee's hair brushed lightly against her cheek and the calming scent of lavender soothed her worries. She breathed in time with Aimee's smooth and steady heartbeat and, after a few moments, felt her anxiety fall away. "How do you always know what I need?"

She felt rather than saw Aimee's smile. "Magic."

"Seriously." She didn't know why she had to know, but suddenly it was very important.

Aimee leaned back and stared deep into her eyes. "The same way you know what I need. Love." She grinned and added, "Oh, and you get this panicked look in your eye when you need a little escape."

Skye opened her mouth to reply, but a loud cry pierced the air. Both of them turned to the kitchen counter and stared at the monitor.

"Speaking of need," Aimee said, "you go. I'll get our drinks and meet you in the dining room."

Skye felt the tension come back the minute she left Aimee and started up the stairs. When she reached the top landing, she broke into a run. Despite Aimee's calm, she still hadn't gotten used to these episodes, and they never failed to bring her to the brink of panic. She rushed into the room and pulled up short at the railing of the huge mahogany baby bed Aimee had insisted on. As she grasped the frame and stared down at the red-faced, mouthy occupant, she silently thanked her wife for buying the most expensive, sturdiest crib on the market.

"Shh," she murmured as she lifted Olivia into her arms. "You're going to wake the people in the next state with your crying."

As she bounced Olivia, the screams subsided into gurgles and grunts. Skye urged them along with aahs and oohs she would only voice in the privacy of her home. Her daughter reduced her to a pile of mush.

Her daughter. Not quite a reality yet, but Parker was sitting downstairs with the paperwork that would make it happen. Two weeks ago when Skye had gotten the call that Olivia was on the way, she'd rushed to Aimee's side and held her hand through every second of her labor. She held Olivia while the doctor cut the cord and spent hours standing outside the hospital nursery, staring at the wonderful new life that she knew would turn theirs upside down. Now it was time to take the final step to adopt her daughter, and she couldn't be more excited. Or more scared.

She rocked Olivia in her arms until she fell back to sleep. Hard to believe the howling baby now basked in peaceful drool. Things could change so drastically in an instant.

Aimee and Parker looked up as she walked into the dining room. Aimee flashed a radiant smile, and Skye stuffed her fear.

"Parker says we can get the home visit done on Tuesday, and we already have a hearing date for next week." Aimee glowed with excitement. She'd been glowing since the moment she'd learned she was pregnant and she'd been giddy the entire time. While she reveled in the excitement of it all, Skye had installed safety locks on every window, cabinet, and door in their home, and read every article Google coughed up on the dangers that could befall an infant.

"Thursday, right?" If she kept saying it, maybe it would sink in.

"Yes. Can you believe it?"

Skye flashed the smile she knew was expected and sat down at the table. "No. That's great news."

The paperwork Parker pushed in front of her appeared blurry, the words floating off the page. For the next half hour, while Parker explained how the hearing on second-parent adoption would work, she managed to grip a pen, and sign and initial more blanks than she had when she and Aimee had refinanced their home. When Parker finally stacked the signed paperwork and placed it in her briefcase, Skye silently congratulated herself on fooling the two of them into thinking she was calm and cool about the situation. But her mind was already ticking ahead to the home visit. First step, get rid of what her mother had always called the machine of death. Her 1995 Harley Softtail.

"Stuart, I can't believe you let her buy that machine of death."

Skye's father's reply was swift and adamant. *"She's an adult and it's her money."*

Skye had listened to the exchange. It was the first time her mother had ever treated her differently than her brothers. The boys in the family all had motorcycles, and no one had ever voiced a concern that they might die in a fiery wreck, but according to her mother, she was doomed to a horrible death if she chose to ride that "monstrosity."

Skye's Harley had been her primary mode of transportation most of her life and she'd never had a wreck, but she wasn't about to take a chance that the caseworker assigned to do the home visit was a worrywart like her mother. She mentally challenged the caseworker to find a single sharp object or toy with small parts, and the only bike present on her visit would be the sparkly purple tricycle with fringe on the handlebars that Olivia would have to wait several years to ride.

Later that afternoon, when she handed over the keys and the title to her Harley, she remembered the first time Aimee had ridden with her. Wearing an expensive tailored suit and Skye's helmet, she'd wrapped her arms around Skye's waist and squeezed the breath out of her as they sped up I-35 from Austin to Round Rock. When they'd stopped at the Harley-Davidson dealership, Aimee squealed and wanted to know when she could ride again. They'd spent an hour at the store while she selected the most stylish helmet, boots, and leather jacket, and then begged to ride again. Her excitement had been intoxicating.

Skye didn't need the bike for excitement. With Aimee, every day was an adventure, and their most exciting adventure was upstairs in a crib, relying on them to keep her safe.

❖

"Tomorrow's the big day." Aimee bounced on the edge of the bed.

Skye held up a finger and strained to listen. That noise again. She picked up the monitor on their nightstand and placed it against her ear. "Shh, can you hear it?"

"Did you just call our daughter an it?"

"Not even. Seriously, Aimee, I swear I heard something in there." She swung her legs off the side of the bed. "I'll go check."

"Uh-uh. I don't think so." Aimee pulled her back down onto

the bed. "I was just with her. She's fine. If you go in there you're going to wake her, and you'll ruin my plans."

Skye recognized the tone and she felt an instant surge of arousal. "You have plans?"

"I've had plans for a very long time, but it's hard to carry out a good plan when you haven't had any sleep. I slept like a baby, no pun intended, after the home visit yesterday, and now I'm ready to implement my strategy."

Skye leaned up on one arm. Aimee was irresistible when she had her mind made up about something. "I might be interested in hearing about your strategy."

Aimee began to slowly unbutton her silk nightshirt. "You'll have to watch and learn. It's more a show than tell kind of thing."

Skye forced herself to wait as her wife slowly stripped down to lacy silk panties. "If your plan is designed to distract me, it's working."

"My plan is designed to make you scream."

"What if we wake Olivia?" Skye glanced at the closed door.

"She's not going to come walking in, if that's what you're worried about." Aimee pointed at the monitor. "If she needs us, she'll be sure to let us know."

"I don't know. As I recall, we can get kind of lost when we're, you know…" The last nine months had been an awkward dance. As Aimee's pregnancy progressed, Skye had become more and more attracted to the glow of her pregnant wife, but ever cautious about the life growing inside her. She'd curtailed her work so she could spend more time by Aimee's side and turned down the more dangerous assignments in favor of the computer searches and paper reviews she normally despised. In the month before Olivia's birth, when Aimee was diagnosed with preeclampsia and on bed rest, she'd started working from home so she could be no more than a few feet away in the event of disaster. After all, the house was full of danger. Stairs, balconies, slick wood floors. She'd do anything to protect her lover, the mother of their child, and "anything" had extended to keeping her hands to herself.

She'd assumed everything would change once Olivia was born. Aimee would be healthy again. She'd resume her regular work schedule, and the only changes to their lives would be bottles and car seats and tiny little clothes to wash. But, if anything, her worry was worse now. Concern about Aimee's health was one thing, but Olivia was tiny and completely without skills. She relied on them for her every need, and she required the kind of protection that could only be provided by a vigilant parent.

"Skye Keaton, do you want to make love to me or not? Because I'm as hot for you as I was the very first time, and I'm not about to let an eight-pound, drooling, screaming mess come between me and my hot wife. If it hadn't been so long, you wouldn't have to say things like 'as I recall.' Now, let's have some torrid sex that neither of us will ever forget."

Aimee had always been able to read her mind. She gasped as Aimee punctuated her demand by yanking Skye's shirt over her head. Skye's breath hitched as the memory of every intimate moment they'd ever shared came rushing back. They could have this and be parents too, right? As Aimee's lips grazed over her nipple, she answered her own question by casting one last look at the monitor on the nightstand before arching into Aimee's embrace.

"Stop fidgeting, you look great."

"I look stupid." Skye stood in front of the full-length mirror and frowned at the image staring back. Wasn't the first time she'd worn a suit, but every time was just as uncomfortable as the last. Too many layers, too many buttons, too much fuss. Every other time had been, like today, for some special occasion, usually something related to Aimee's successful real estate business or one of her many social causes: black-tie dinner, office holiday party, dinner with Aimee's wealthy and very formal Highland Park parents. Today, she'd wear whatever it took for the judge to think she was worthy.

"You can take it off the minute we get home."

"What about the party?" While they were at the courthouse, caterers would be preparing their fete in celebration of Olivia officially belonging to both of them.

"What about it? You can wear cut-offs and an old T-shirt, for all I care. And if you think Olivia will care, you haven't been paying attention. She spends most of her time in a onesie." Aimee lifted Olivia and held her up in the air. "But not today, right, little one? Everyone's dressed up today!"

Olivia, covered in pink lace and ribbon, screamed with delight as Aimee whirled her around the room. Skye smiled on the outside, but inwardly she strained against the image of Olivia falling through the air and landing with a thud on the hardwood floor.

Aimee's sharp voice jerked her from her fatalist imaginings. "Skye, I'm not going to drop our daughter. And if you don't wipe that look of horror off your face, the judge is going to think we're crazy and give Olivia to a whole different set of parents."

So much for her ability to mask her emotions. "He might do that anyway. Parker isn't a family law attorney. Maybe we should have hired someone else."

"You said yourself she's one of the smartest people you know. She consulted with a board-certified family law specialist about our case. She found a judge who has granted over a dozen second-parent adoptions, and she's like family." Aimee set Olivia back in her crib. When she turned, Skye recognized the formidable, hands-on-hips, stern-jaw look and braced for a rant.

"I think you're amazing. Hell, I married you. The caseworker couldn't have written a better report and I think if I weren't around, she'd marry you herself. If you're having second thoughts about," she jerked her head in the direction of Olivia's crib, "speak now or forever hold your peace."

Pain lanced Skye's heart and she swept Aimee into her arms. "No, no, no," she murmured into her ear. "No second thoughts. Not a one. It's just…I feel so out of sorts. Like I don't have a clue what I'm doing." She waved at the crib. "She's so tiny. Helpless. If anything ever happened to her, I don't know what I'd do."

"Is that why our house is suddenly Fort Knox? I locked myself in the bathroom yesterday because I couldn't figure out how to turn the handle with the huge rubber thing you've installed. You realize it's going to be a while before she can even reach drawers and door handles and outlets, right?"

Skye felt her face redden. "I know, but there was the home visit and I didn't want the caseworker to think I was irresponsible. I mean, she knew I work as a private investigator and I'm sure she had some preconceived notions about that."

"Is that why you sold your bike?"

"What?" She hadn't mentioned the sale to Aimee. She'd had a feeling she might get flack for it.

"Parker told me."

"Some attorney she is. Way to keep information confidential."

"Shut up," Aimee said. "She's our friend. I think she was half-mortified and half-impressed that, how did she put it? That you were acting like an adult. You should've told me. That bike was the first thing I noticed about you."

Skye flashed on a memory. She had just ridden up Cedar Springs and parked outside Hunky's, a popular hamburger joint. While she contemplated whether she wanted to spend her last few bucks on lunch, a gorgeous blonde in a fancy SUV pulled up beside her and practically undressed her with her eyes. Never in a million years did Skye expect she would one day marry that woman and have a baby with her, but here she was.

Things change. Giving up the bike had been the right thing to do.

❖

The courtroom was already packed when they arrived. Skye scanned the room. Aimee's family and hers lined the first two rows. The rest of the seats were filled with their family of choice. Assistant District Attorney Cory Lance and her partner Serena Washington. Parker's wife, Morgan Bradley. Aimee's best friend, Mackenzie Lewis, and her partner Dr. Jordan Wagner. Megan and Haley.

She took her seat with Aimee and Olivia next to Parker at one of the tables inside the court railing. She was no stranger to the courtroom, having testified both as a cop and more recently as a private investigator, but today was different. Today she was on trial, or at least her fitness as a parent was. Parker had assured her Judge Lucas was fair and friendly, but until he signed the order stating Olivia was legally hers, she wouldn't be able to breathe.

When the judge took the bench, Parker offered the motion for second-parent adoption, the home study, and letters in support. Judge Lucas commented on the glowing report from the caseworker, said a few words in legalese, smacked his gavel, and then asked if he could be included in the first official family photo. As he made his way toward them, Skye looked from Parker to Aimee and back again, certain she'd missed something. The whole thing had lasted no more than fifteen minutes.

"Close your mouth, Keaton," Parker said, lightly punching her in the arm. "It's official. Olivia has two moms."

Skye turned to Aimee, who held their sleeping daughter, who was apparently immune to the sound of smacking gavels. "It's for real."

Aimee whispered in her ear, her breath soft and sweet. "It was always for real. It's just legal now." Aimee handed Olivia into her arms as the judge took his place beside them for the photo. "Now wake up your daughter. I have a feeling this is the first of many pictures today."

Almost an hour later they'd finally managed to please everyone's need for photos and were in the car on the way home for the party. Skye pulled into the driveway and reached for the garage door opener, but Aimee placed a hand on hers. "Park in the driveway for now."

"Why? Didn't you just get the car washed?"

"Trust me. I cleared out some space for the caterers to put their equipment, and there's nowhere for you to park in there."

Skye shook her head. "You know they could have figured out what to do with their own stuff." Aimee was a socialite on the surface, but she had never been above chipping in on a project, and this party had been quite the undertaking. "But I love you for making this day special." She parked the car and kissed Aimee on the lips. "We'd better get inside. Our guests will be arriving soon."

They worked together to get Olivia out of the car seat. It became easier every time. As they stepped though the side door to the garage, Aimee pulled Skye into an embrace.

"I want to talk to you about something."

"Here in the dark? Sounds ominous." Skye couldn't quite read Aimee's tone.

Aimee cast a look down at Olivia. "I just want you to know that there's no one I'd rather spend the rest of my life with. And no one I'd want to raise this little girl with. You are going to be, you already are, a wonderful mother."

"Okay." Skye stretched out the word, still uncertain where this was going.

"But as much as I want you to keep her safe, I also want you to challenge her. One of the things I love about you the most is your fearlessness. I want her to learn that from you, whether you are teaching her to ride this," she flicked on the light switch and gestured to the sparkly purple tricycle in the corner, "or this."

Following where Aimee pointed, Skye shook her head in disbelief. A Harley—her Harley stood in the center of the garage with a big red bow on the seat.

Aimee kissed her. "I have a feeling Olivia is going to take after you in a lot of ways—she's already told me she was born to ride."

About the Author

Carsen Taite's goal as an author is to spin tales with plot lines as interesting as the cases she encountered in her career as a criminal defense lawyer. She is the award-winning author of over two dozen novels of romance and romantic intrigue, including the Luca Bennett Bounty Hunter series, the Lone Star Law series, the Legal Affairs romances, and the Courting Danger series.

Books Available From Bold Strokes Books

A Fox in Shadow by Jane Fletcher. Cassie's mission is to add new territory to the Kavillian empire—murder, betrayal, war, and the clash of cultures ensue. (978-1-63679-142-5)

Embracing the Moon by Jeannie Levig. Just as Gwen and Taylor are exploring the new love they've found, the present and past collide, threatening the future they long to share. (978-1-63555-462-5)

Forever Comes in Threes by D. Jackson Leigh. Efficiency expert Perry Chandler's ordered life is upended when she inherits three busy terriers, and the woman she's referred to for help turns out to be her bitter podcast rival, the very sexy Dr. Ming Lee. (978-1-63679-169-2)

Heckin' Lewd: Trans and Nonbinary Erotica, edited by Mx. Nillin Lore. If you want smutty, fearless, gender diverse erotica written by affirming own-voices folks who get it, then this is the book you've been looking for! (978-1-63679-240-8)

Missed Conception by Joy Argento. Maggie Walsh wants a relationship with Cassidy, the daughter she's only just discovered she has due to an in vitro mix-up. Heat kindles between Maggie and Cassidy's mother in a way neither expects. (978-1-63679-146-3)

Private Equity by Elle Spencer. Cassidy Bennett spends an unexpected evening at a lesbian nightclub with her notoriously reserved and demanding boss, Julia. After seeing a different side of Julia, Cassidy can't seem to shake her desire to know more. (978-1-63679-180-7)

Racing the Dawn by Sandra Barrett. After narrowly escaping a house fire, vampire Jade Murphy is unexpectedly intrigued by gorgeous firefighter Beth Jenssen, and her undead existence might just be perking up a bit. (978-1-63679-271-2)

Reclaiming Love by Amanda Radley. Sarah's tiny white lie means somehow convincing Pippa to pretend to be her girlfriend. Only the more time they spend faking it, the more real it feels. (978-1-63679-144-9)

Sol Cycle by Kimberly Cooper Griffin. An encounter in a park brings Ang and Krista together, but when Ang's attempts to help Krista go spectacularly wrong, their passion for each other might not be enough. (978-1-63679-137-1)

Trial and Error by Carsen Taite. Attorney Franco Rossi and Judge Nina Aguilar's reunion is fraught with courtroom conflict, undeniable chemistry, and danger. (978-1-63555-863-0)

A Long Way to Fall by Elle Spencer. A ski lodge, two strong-willed women, and a family feud that brings them together, but will it also tear them apart? (978-1-63679-005-3)

Forever by Kris Bryant. When Savannah Edwards is invited to be the next bachelorette on the dating show *When Sparks Fly*, she'll show the world that finding true love on television can happen. (978-1-63679-029-9)

. **Ice on Wheels** by Aurora Rey. All's fair in love and roller derby. That's Riley Fauchet's motto, until a new job lands her at the same company—and on the same team—as her rival Brooke Landry, the frosty jammer for the Big Easy Bruisers. (978-1-63679-179-1)

Perfect Rivalry by Radclyffe. Two women set out to win the same career-making goal, but it's love that may turn out to be the final prize. (978-1-63679-216-3)

Something to Talk About by Ronica Black. Can quiet ranch owner Corey Durand give up her peaceful life and allow her feisty new neighbor into her heart? Or will past loss, present suitors, and town gossip ruin a long-awaited chance at love? (978-1-63679-114-2)

With a Minor in Murder by Karis Walsh. In the world of academia, police officer Clare Sawyer and professor Libby Hart team up to solve a murder. (978-1-63679-186-9)

Writer's Block by Ali Vali. Wyatt and Hayley might be made for each other if only they can get through nosy neighbors, the historic society, at-odds future plans, and all the secrets hidden in Wyatt's walls. (978-1-63679-021-3)